Sunset Tides

Pittsburgh

SUNSET TIDES

ANJ Press, First edition. OCTOBER 2022.

Copyright © 2022 Amelia Addler.

Written by Amelia Addler.

Cover design by CrocoDesigns

Maps by MistyBeee

For the courage to look within

Recap and Introduction to *Sunset Tides*

Welcome back to Orcas Island! In the first two books in the series, we met Claire Cooke and her three daughters, Lucy, Lillian, and Rose.

Their story started with tragedy nearly thirty years ago when a plane crash claimed the lives of Claire's family, including her parents and her sister, the girls' biological mother Holly.

At the time, Claire believed her twin sister Becca had also died in the crash. She had no one to lean on, and she adopted her sister Holly's three girls and rebuilt their lives. She worked hard at her job as a paralegal and always put the girls first.

It wasn't until Claire hit fifty-two that she did something entirely for herself. The girls' uncle had left her a six-million-dollar inheritance, which she put toward buying the Grand Madrona Hotel on Orcas Island.

From there, things got a bit wild. Claire discovered that years ago, her twin sister Becca had had a son – Marty – and he was wanted by the FBI. He managed to clear his name and decided to move to the island, at which point he started the hunt for his biological mom, Becca.

Marty found out that Becca was alive, which resulted in a tearful reunion between the sisters. Marty also met the love of his life – Emma – and found a way to make peace with his mom.

In book three, we join Lucy in her new, calm life on the island working at a local farm. That is, until a handsome New Yorker shows up just as both the farm and the hotel end up in hot water...

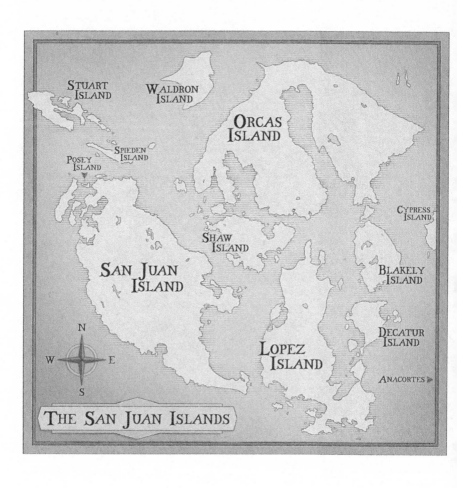

STUART
ISLAND

WALDRON
ISLAND

ORCAS
ISLAND

POSEY
ISLAND

SPIEDEN
ISLAND

CYPRESS
ISLAND

SHAW
ISLAND

SAN JUAN
ISLAND

BLAKELY
ISLAND

DECATUR
ISLAND

N

W ——————— E

S

LOPEZ
ISLAND

ANACORTES ▶

THE SAN JUAN ISLANDS

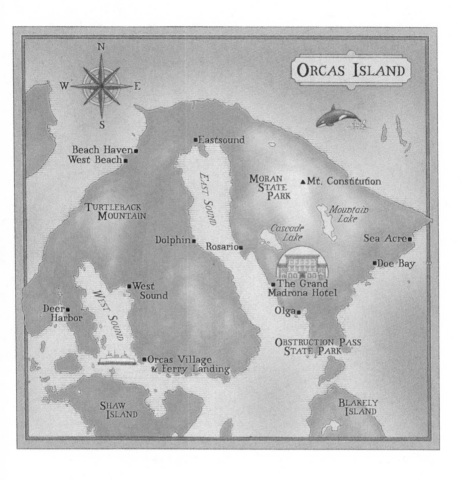

Chapter One

There was no reason to be unhappy. It was a nice day, particularly for February, with clear blue skies and even a bit of sunshine. Lucy woke feeling a bit dull, but it wasn't something to dwell on.

If she looked hard enough, there was plenty of joy to be found. The new jacket she'd ordered arrived early, and the medium, which reviews said ran small, fit perfectly.

Maybe she'd spent more on it than she should have, but it was cute, reasonably warm, and made her feel chic. What more could she ask from a jacket?

She got to work fifteen minutes late that morning, but as usual, no one seemed to notice. Her boss Fiona was laid back, and the customers had an innate understanding that the little farm shop on Orcas Island didn't run on "city" time.

The farm itself looked like something off of a postcard – picturesque fields, rows of apple trees and little goats running amok. It was the perfect place to work. Lucy had full control over running the shop at Grindstone Farm. Her boss was happy with her, the customers were happy with her, even the goats were happy with her.

So why, with no reason to be unhappy, was she *so* unhappy? And why did she feel the irresistible urge to quit?

The feeling first appeared a few months ago. It started small and innocuous, a leaky sink in her mind, with her wondering if she could really keep working at the farm long-term. It was just a few thoughts, a dripping in the distance that was annoying, but nothing she couldn't ignore.

Then three months in, she let her mind wander a bit too far and she stepped into a deep puddle of doubt, panicking that she was wasting her life and had no future at the farm.

That was just one time, though, and Lucy managed to hastily hurry along like nothing had happened.

It was easy enough to do because people *liked* her at Grindstone. Heck, she even liked herself at this job. She couldn't say that for any of the last half dozen jobs she'd had. On top of that, she was good at this job. Lucy had improved the farm's online presence by doing everything from taking new pictures to promoting events to advertising what they had for sale. Their online profits were up seventy percent since she'd taken over.

The rest of the employees made her feel like part of the family. They were such *nice* people, too, people who worked hard, had lovely families, and somehow balanced in hobbies. They were happy.

Lucy wanted to be happy.

Yet six months in, the incessant dripping in the back of her mind was getting to her. She had trouble focusing on books and even TV shows seemed drab. At the end of the day, she'd sit and stare mindlessly at her phone, exhausted but unable to sleep.

She was getting bags under her eyes from the lack of sleep. Wrinkles had sprouted up around the bags, too, like scaffolding around a crumbling building. Lucy couldn't afford the concealer to handle it all.

That morning, staring at her tired face in the reflection of a cookie-scented candle, Lucy realized she had to face the truth: it was time to move on.

Once her mind was made up, she moved fast. She finished the inventory and packed up the newest online orders, then sat behind the register and scrolled through job postings on her phone. She considered applying to a handful, but Lucy wasn't sure what she was looking for, but she felt she'd know it when she saw it. Hesitation drifted in. Maybe she should take her time to find the right job?

"It's nice to see a friendly face today," said a man's voice.

Lucy looked up from her phone and smiled reflexively. "Hi Mr. Green. How's it going?"

"Oh pretty good, Lucy, pretty good. Just needed to grab some eggs."

She nodded, bagging them for him. "No problem. Anything else we can do for you today?"

He set a brown paper bag on the counter. "I came from the bakery in Eastsound and they'd just pulled a tray of apple turnovers out of the oven. I got you one. I know they're your favorite."

"That is so sweet!" Lucy counted out his change before picking up the small bag. "Thank you."

He nodded. "Take care."

Sigh.

Such a sweet man. Sometimes he came in with his wife. They'd been married for forty-six years, which Lucy knew because Mrs. Green repeated it, over and over.

The bag in her hand smelled like cinnamon and happiness, and she could feel the warmth radiating into her palm. It was exceedingly kind of Mr. Green to get something for her, though it wasn't all that unusual for one of their regulars to be thoughtful like that.

The regulars. Hah. Lucy had never stayed anywhere long enough to become a regular. It seemed like an odd thing to do.

Yet somehow, she'd become the other side of the "regular" coin. Mr. Green knew she liked – no, loved – apple turnovers. Why did she talk so much? For a customer to know enough about her to get the most delightful treat on a whim surely meant she needed to move on and –

She pulled it from the crinkling paper and took a bite.

Ugh. The pastry was thin and flaky, the apple sliced and softened to a perfect crisp. It was heavenly and absolutely perfect.

Too perfect.

Yeah. It was time to go, sooner rather than later. If she stuck around any longer, she'd end up half a century into a marriage repeating the same line, over and over.

She was too young for that!

The jig was up. It was time to move on. Lucy was sure of it.

Not before she finished the apple turnover, though. She wasn't an animal.

Sunset Tides

Chapter Two

Lucy managed to put off quitting until the end of the day. As she closed the shop, she told herself it was now or never. There was no use in putting off quitting or dragging it out. Sleeping on it would only prolong her dread, and she'd quit enough jobs to know the best way to do it: quickly, with no warning, like ripping off a band-aid.

It was always hard to say goodbye, especially when she had a boss she liked. Her last boss had made it hard to quit, but for a *unique* reason. They'd had a brief romantic liaison, and after that went south, he'd avoided her like a hornet at a picnic. When she'd finally had a chance to hand in her notice, it was actually quite fun.

This time wouldn't be fun.

She made the walk to Fiona's office, which was housed in a trailer on the property. Lucy decided against warning her she was coming. Fiona might get suspicious, then ask her if she was quitting, then prepare a whole spiel to convince her to stay. Lucy was always susceptible to convincing, so she didn't want that possibility in the air.

The walk to the trailer was shorter than usual, and once she got there, she took a deep breath and knocked on the door.

Fiona yelled out, "Come in!"

Lucy stumbled inside, tripping on a chair placed in front of the door. She managed to catch herself before she fell, annoyed to see the chair had been moved to make room for a guest. A *male* guest.

"I didn't realize you were meeting with someone," she said. "Is now not a good time?"

Fiona shook her head. "It's fine." Her voice was small and tired. Her hair was messed up, too, and half of the collar on her flannel shirt was popped.

Yeesh. What had happened to Fiona?

The guy who'd been occupying the chair stood and offered Lucy a handshake, and she accepted, taking a step back as she did. He towered over her, looking entirely out of place in his tightly tailored black suit.

"Hi there, I'm Rob. It's nice to meet you."

She stared up at his face. It was flawless – tanned, dimpled, like that of a collegiate athlete in a recruitment pamphlet, or an airbrushed model in an overpriced cologne ad. His overly-humble smile annoyed her.

"Hi, I'm Lucy. Nice to meet you." She turned to Fiona. "I didn't mean to interrupt. I can come back tomorrow."

"Please, it's not a problem. What's up?"

Lucy shot a wary look at Rob, who continued standing over her and smiling.

She wished he would sit down. Or better yet, leave. "No, it's okay. It's kind of private."

Rob put his hands up. "Hey, I can take a hint, I'll just – "

Fiona let out a gasp. "You're quitting, aren't you?"

"No!" Lucy said, her voice jumping an octave.

"It's okay. You'd be right to do it." Fiona pressed her eyes with her fingers before looking up.

Lucy had never seen her so frazzled. "What's going on? Is this guy threatening you?"

Rob let out a forced laugh. "Whoa, whoa. No, I'm not – ."

"No." Fiona let out a sigh. "He's not threatening me."

"I'm here with an opportunity," he said.

Lucy crossed her arms. He was pretty big, but she thought she might be able to take him. At the very least, the two of them could take him, if Fiona stopped acting so defeated.

Unless he had some sort of weapon hidden in that custom-stitched suit. Then it would be tough. Maybe Lucy could get the biting farm donkey on her side. He was a surprisingly formidable foe, that donkey. He'd bitten her on her first day. That had been the low point of working here, actually...

"Rob is here because the farm's in trouble. I thought we could pull it together, but it's been three years and..."

"What kind of trouble?" asked Lucy.

"Oh," she let out a long-winded laugh. "Just a little over a million dollars' worth of trouble."

Lucy raised her eyebrows. "Dang."

"So now is really the perfect time for you to find a new job," she added.

Rob shot Lucy an unconvincingly sympathetic smile.

She turned from him and took a seat. "I'm not going anywhere. How did this happen?"

Chapter Three

Rob needed alone time with Fiona, but this intrusion by Lucy was nothing he couldn't handle. A small bump in the road.

He reached for his briefcase. "I'd be happy to treat you to dinner tonight, Fiona, if that would be better?"

"No, no." Lucy said, sitting back in her seat. "Let's talk now."

Fiona shrugged her shoulders.

The woman had given up. That was fine. It'd be easier to get her to buy into his plan that way.

He took a seat. "I have a packet of figures here, but I don't want to bore you with too many numbers. Basically, if Carriageway Holdings goes forward with bankruptcy – "

"Who is Carriageway Holdings?" Lucy asked.

"It's a long story – it's the company that bought the farm three years ago," Fiona said.

Rob continued. "If they do declare bankruptcy, we have what we call a nightmare scenario."

Lucy snatched a packet out of his hand. "A nightmare for you, or for us?"

He smiled. She was surprisingly passionate about the farm going bankrupt, considering she'd quite obviously just tried to quit. "I'd hate to see it. Carriageway would likely auction off the farm's assets one by one – the buildings, the equipment, even the animals."

And the land. Especially the land. What a waste to let all of these prime acres be auctioned off.

Fiona let out a groan. "That is my nightmare."

"But," he swooped in, leaning forward and leading Fiona to page three of the packet, "if you allow my company to come in and reorganize the deal, that won't happen. We can restructure, rebuild, and make the farm even better than before."

Rob paused. He'd learned long ago to always present the worst option first, then follow with a much better sounding option. Who wouldn't like a little rebuilding and restructuring? It sounded harmless.

Of course, his company wasn't harmless. No one made money saving farms, and Grindstone Farm wasn't special. That wasn't something they needed to know, though.

"Yeah," Fiona said, flipping through the pages. "This sounds great, but how am I supposed to convince them to sell to you?"

Lucy interrupted. "Hang on. I thought you were in charge, Fiona?"

She shook her head. "Not with things like this."

Rob cut in. "Yet still, you're an important member of Grindstone. The guys at Carriageway aren't farmers – they don't understand the value of century-old apple tree lines or the aged whiskey in your cellar."

"No one cares about that," Fiona said glumly.

"Our customers do," Lucy snapped, shooting Rob a look.

That one was too defensive. He needed to be more convincing. "Of course, and that's what Carriageway doesn't understand. They also don't understand how difficult it'll be to sell everything off. They may not recoup their costs, and all they want to do is cut and run."

Lucy narrowed her eyes. "How long has this one million dollar problem been hanging over your head, Fiona?"

"Since Harry sold the farm. Three years. I'll tell you about it later."

Lucy was killing Rob's pitch with her questions. He kept a synthetic smile on his face, but he wanted nothing more than to shut this pushy woman out of the office and lock the door.

"We can go over the details soon," he said, "but I wanted to introduce myself and let you know there are other options. Options that could save the farm."

"What company do you work for?" asked Lucy.

"It's called OSS. Obringer, Sterling and Sullivan."

"Sounds local," she said with a smile.

Ah, sarcasm. A tool for the witless. "We're based out of New York City, but we have an office in Seattle."

"New York City." She sat back and let out a deep breath. "You must know a lot about farms."

"I can't claim I do, but I'm willing to learn. We care a lot about small businesses."

Lucy nodded. "Right. What other small businesses have you saved?"

"Lucy," Fiona said in a low voice. "He's not the enemy."

She shrugged. "He may not be the enemy, but it doesn't look like he could muck out a stall in that suit."

Rob knew he shouldn't have worn a suit. He just hadn't had time to change when he'd gotten to this miserable island. As far as he was concerned, it was on the other end of the world, and on top of that, the ferry he'd taken was an hour late.

Time to call Lucy on her bluff. "I'd be happy to help in the stalls." He stood and removed his suit jacket, laying it on the chair.

"Please. You don't have to do that," Fiona said, waving a hand for him to sit down. "This is very interesting, Rob. I'm going to talk to Alan from Carriageway and see what he thinks."

"That's all I ask. And if you need any help in the barn – "

"No." Fiona smiled for the first time. "That's kind of you, but thank you."

Rob could feel Lucy's eyes on him. He shot her a look and shrugged his shoulders. "The offer is always on the table."

Lucy cleared her throat and stood, announcing, "Well, you look exhausted, Fiona, so I'll leave you in peace. I can show Rob out."

Now she was kicking him out! She was going from rude to outright irritating.

No need to show his annoyance, though. Rob smiled. "Thanks, Lucy. I'll stop by tomorrow. I've got some calls to make and – "

"Of course!" Lucy opened the door, motioning for Rob to step through.

He cleared his throat. "You have my card. Please feel free to reach out any time of day. I have a small office on the island and _ "

Lucy cut him off. "Thanks a bunch, Rob. Let me show you to your car."

"Have a nice day," he said, grabbing his jacket. "We'll be in touch."

Chapter Four

They walked through the tip of the apple orchards, past the distillery and on to the barn. Lucy stopped and pointed at the open barn door.

"Last chance if you'd like to muck a stall."

Rob flashed what he surely thought was an award-winning smile. "Not today. Maybe next time."

Lucy smiled back, though with less charm and more open disdain. It may have been closer to a sneer than a smile, but she couldn't be bothered with worrying about these things. "Sure. The parking lot is right over there. I assume that's your Audi out front?"

"Yes." He paused. "Well, it's not mine. It's a rental. A company rental."

"Right. Have a nice day, Rob." She turned and walked toward the barn, slipping inside and watching from a window as he got into his car.

Lucy stared. He was just sitting there. She couldn't make out what he was doing. Why wasn't he leaving? Was he calling back to the New York office to tell his friends what suckers they were? To talk about the simple country bumpkins he was going to trick into some scheme?

She didn't know *what* the scheme was, exactly, but it seemed like the most likely option. Lucy glared at him, not realizing her breath was fogging up the window. She wiped it clean just as he started his car and pulled out of the parking spot.

"Good riddance," she muttered.

A bleat rang out behind her and Lucy jumped at the sound. She'd thought she was alone. Apparently one of the goats had found her. "Go back outside, bud. I don't have anything for you."

He looked up at her with his big eyes, his ears flopping as he walked closer. He was a stunner, and one of her favorites – an adorable little guy with white fur and black spots and speckles, always hopping and bleating and causing a scene. She watched as he jumped on top of an overturned bucket, balancing expertly, and calling out with another bleat.

Lucy laughed. There was nothing cuter than a baby goat. "Goofball."

She left the barn and rushed back to Fiona's trailer. Thankfully, the door wasn't locked and Lucy barged in yelling, "I'm back!"

Fiona was still sitting at her desk. She looked up at Lucy and let out a heavy sigh. "I thought you were going to let me rest."

"I got that guy out of your office for you." She plopped down in a seat. "You're welcome."

Fiona shrugged. "He might be our best option."

"How is that possible? How did the farm get into so much debt? I thought we were doing really well."

"We have been doing really well," Fiona said. "Better than ever, actually."

"Then what happened?"

Fiona stood, walking to the mini refrigerator in the corner of the trailer. She pulled out a glass jug of fresh apple juice. "Would you like some?"

"No thanks." Lucy paused. "Actually, yes please." She couldn't resist the stuff. That was one of the problems with working at Grindstone Farm – her sugar consumption had gone through the roof.

Fiona poured two glasses and handed one to Lucy. "You never had a chance to meet him, but the old owner of the farm was a guy named Harry."

"I've seen his pictures. The guy that was always in overalls?"

Fiona nodded. "Yeah. He was great. His parents had owned the farm before him, but they'd just had the orchards. When he took over, he bought more land, added the distillery, and refurbished the barn. He practically had to rebuild it from the ground up."

Lucy took a sip of juice. It was the perfect blend of sweet and tart. Nothing she got at the grocery store ever tasted anywhere near this good. The farm had forever ruined her for apple juice. "Did he have a gambling problem or something?"

"No, nothing like that." Fiona sat down again. "He'd always joked that he planned to die working out on the farm, but it didn't end up that way. Right after his seventy-eighth birthday, he was diagnosed with lung cancer."

"Aw man." The guy looked so pleasant in the pictures, almost like a caricature of what she imagined a sweet old farmer would be.

A pang of guilt drifted over Lucy. She shouldn't have made that gambling joke about the poor guy.

"Harry didn't let it get him down, but he decided he wanted to spend his remaining time doing something he'd always dreamed of: touring the world's farms."

Lucy laughed. "You're kidding. That was his dream?"

She nodded. "Oh yes. He'd traveled quite a bit in his life, but it was always limited because he worked so much on the farm. He visited Scotland to tour whiskey distilleries, and spent some time in French vineyards and wineries. It was his favorite thing to do. Back when he was young, in his fifties, he'd gotten to know some of the world's top apple breeders. He talked about it all the time."

"Apple breeding! That's a thing?"

"Yes," Fiona said. "How else do you think we created the best apples?"

Lucy had learned the names of their top varieties, but she hadn't thought much of it. Apparently, apples were a serious science.

Fiona continued. "But Harry wanted to do more, and for that reason, he was in a hurry to sell the farm."

"To this Carriageway Holdings company?"

"Yes. I don't blame him for it," Fiona said. "I really don't. He put the farm up for sale, and the offers he got were too low.

At the time, Grindstone was bringing in about fifty thousand dollars of profit every year."

Lucy paused. She knew farms typically had low profit margins, which was wild considering how hard the farmers worked year-round. "That's pretty good, isn't it?"

"For a farm, yes, but Harry was never money-focused. He'd hardly made a profit most years before that, so there just wasn't much interest in buying the farm. He got an offer for about double the farm's yearly profit. It wasn't bad, exactly, but it wasn't enough to pay for his treatments and traveling."

"I see."

"Then, out of the blue, Carriageway Holdings approached him. They offered to pay one and a half *million* dollars for the farm."

Lucy's mouth popped open. "Whoa. That's awesome." She paused. "What was the catch?"

"That was what I didn't understand. I told Harry I was worried that they had plans to do something drastic, like sell the land for development, but he assured me that wasn't the case. He signed the deal, and off he went."

Lucy frowned. "I'm still not getting what happened."

Fiona smiled, finishing her juice. "It wasn't obvious at first. It all seemed fine until the first payments were due."

"What payments?"

"Carriageway is what they call a private equity firm. They're not farm people – Rob was right about that. They're business people. They bought the farm with something called a leveraged buyout."

Leveraged buyout. That reminded her of an economics class she'd failed during her brief stint in college. Lucy could feel her eyes glazing over. "I'm sorry, I'm going to try really hard to listen to you, but it already feels like I'm losing that battle."

Fiona laughed. "It took me a while to understand this whole thing. I think they make it complicated on purpose so regular people can't figure out what's going on."

"Rude."

"I know." Fiona stood up and picked up a marker for the dry erase board behind her desk. "Basically, the reason Carriageway were able to offer so much money was because they went to a bank and said, 'Hey, we've got this great farm that's bringing in fifty thousand a year, but with us in charge, it'll bring in half a million a year.'"

"*What!*" Lucy shook her head. "Don't tell me the bank believed them."

"Oh, not only did they believe them, they gave them a loan for one and a half million dollars."

Lucy let out a huff. She didn't know much about farming, but she knew Carriageway's proposal made no sense. That sort of profit was unheard of. "That's insane."

"I know. Carriageway listed all of Grindstone's assets – the distillery, the land, the orchards – and put them on the line for the loan, like collateral. Because of all the collateral, Carriageway only had to pay three hundred thousand dollars for the whole deal."

Lucy frowned. "What's that, like twenty percent? Like a mortgage?"

"Exactly, only better, because they got to keep all of the profits that Grindstone Farm made, year after year. Even though we increased our profits to over two hundred thousand dollars this year – "

"Which is incredible."

Fiona offered her a weak smile. "Thanks. It felt incredible. We've done everything and more, but it still wasn't enough to pay Carriageway and cover the interest on the loan. Every year, we just fell deeper and deeper into debt. Three weeks ago, Carriageway told me they're ready to declare bankruptcy."

"Wow." Lucy let out a puff of air. "So they've lost a lot of money, too."

"No, that's the scummy thing. They've made over a half a million dollars doing *nothing*. They send someone out every quarter to tell us to keep up the good work. Until recently, of course, when they told me they're planning to declare Grindstone Farm bankrupt."

"How can they do that?" Lucy could feel the rage building in her chest. The nerve of these guys! Milking a farm for all they could, then sinking it like it was nothing. Disgusting.

"That's their business model. From what I can tell, they have almost thirty companies like this. Not all of them are farms, some are shops, factories..."

"I can't believe they're allowed to do this."

"I couldn't either, but here we are, living it. No matter what we do, we can't pay off this loan. That much I've accepted."

"So what? You're just going to give up? Let the farm be sold off for parts?"

She let out a sigh. "What else am I supposed to do? When Rob contacted me, I thought his company might be able to keep things going for a bit longer. The way he explains it, if OSS takes over the debt they can restructure it, and we may not need to pay as much."

How generous of him. Yet somehow Lucy didn't think Rob looked like a philanthropist.

She narrowed her eyes. "Why would they do that? Out of the goodness of their hearts?"

"I don't know." Fiona leaned forward, resting her face in her hands. "I'm trying to figure that out."

Lucy didn't trust that guy as far as she could throw him, and she couldn't throw him anywhere, because he was huge. She'd considered it carefully when she thought she was going to have to fight him. "I'm going to come up with something, Fiona. We're not going to let them walk all over us like this."

Fiona picked her head up. "Oh, the confidence of the young. How I miss it."

Lucy downed the rest of her apple juice and stood. "Am I young now? You don't need to flatter me. I'm going to help either way."

She scoffed. "You'll be coming in tomorrow, then?"

"Of course! And all weekend, too. We'll figure something out. We can't be the first farm this has happened to."

Fiona shook her head. "We most certainly are not."

"So there must be a way," Lucy said. "I'll see you bright and early."

Fiona gave her a thumbs up. "Got it."

Lucy practically ran out of the trailer, a fire burning in her chest.

Chapter Five

It had been over a week since Claire had seen Lucy. Normally, Lucy stopped by at least every other day to say hello, or to have dinner at the hotel. It was highly unusual for her to disappear like this.

Claire called her to check in and Lucy apologized, saying she didn't have time to talk. She said something about the "big things" she was doing at Grindstone Farm, but she had no time to explain what that meant.

At the end of the week, Claire decided to head over to the farm and find out for herself. She finished up at the hotel early and told Chip she'd catch up with him later.

"Cutting out early? On a Friday?" Chip sat back, his mouth open in mock surprise. "What do you think this is, a low rent motel?"

She laughed. "I'm leaving The Grand Madrona in your capable hands."

"But we *need* you," he said with a groan. "The chef wants us to try his new menu and wine pairings tonight. You know I'm terrible with pairings."

Claire reached over and patted him on the shoulder. "You really are. You should try to pay attention when he talks about flavors."

Chip shook his head. "I can't do it. I need your help."

She smiled and pulled her coat on. He'd been so particular about their weekends recently.

Was she making him feel neglected? Claire didn't think she'd been busier than usual, though she did go to that conference on the mainland last week. He must've missed her more than she realized. "How about we do it tomorrow night?"

He thought on this for a moment. "Okay. Deal."

She gave him a kiss and rushed out to her car. The drive over to the farm wasn't long, and when she got there, she started her search for Lucy in the tasting room.

It was busy for a rainy winter's day, and Claire couldn't see Lucy anywhere. She was pleased, however, when she spotted Marty and Emma across the room.

"I didn't expect to see you today," Marty said as she walked over. He'd just taken a large bite of apple pie and was struggling to contain it as he talked and chewed. "Did Lucy order you here too?"

"She didn't, but I had to stop by. I'm so curious about what she's up to. Why is she ordering you around?"

Emma looked up, a smile on her face. "I didn't get any orders. I'm here for moral support."

"That's nice of you!" Claire meant it.

She missed working with Emma. Ever since she'd gotten full-time work as a nanny with Marty's boss, Emma no longer worked weekend hours at the hotel. Her smiling presence was sorely missed. Even Gigi, who had never skipped an opportunity to pick on Emma, complained about wanting her to come back.

Marty took a sip of water and fully cleared his mouth of pie. "Consider yourselves lucky. Lucy has a new cause, and she's taking no prisoners."

"A new cause?" Claire took a seat. It wasn't unlike Lucy to get swept up in things. She was passionate, and ever since she had been a kid, she'd gone through phases and cycles. Lucy vacillated between being unbelievably excited and unbearably bored.

"She's trying to save Grindstone Farm from bankruptcy," Emma explained.

"Oh!" Claire laughed. That was unexpected. "How does she plan to do that?"

Marty took another enormous bite of pie before answering. "It's a long shot. I mean, I don't know. Doesn't seem possible, but – " He started coughing.

Emma patted him on the back. "Slow down! We can get more pie!"

He shook his head. "No, please don't let me have any more pie."

"The farm is over a million dollars in debt," Emma said. "I'm not sure how it happened."

"They were bought by a private equity firm," Marty interjected, mostly recovered from his coughing fit. "A leveraged buyout. Have you heard of that before?"

Claire nodded. "They were all the rage in the eighties."

"Ah, so it's a retro business practice?" Marty said with a smile.

Claire pretended to be offended, putting a hand to her chest. "It's not retro. It's – I don't know, modern, apparently!"

"Quite modern," Emma said, shooting Marty a look. "Lucy said she needs to raise money so she can buy the farm back at auction."

Claire let out a breath. That seemed ambitious, even for Lucy.

Before she could comment, Lucy swooped in, her cheeks flushed pink and her eyes wide and bright. "Hey! It's so good to see you all!"

Claire stood and gave her a hug. "It's good to see you, too. Can you sit with us for a minute?"

Lucy shook her head. "There's no time for that, and honestly, I'm disappointed in Marty for sitting here, stuffing pie in his face, when he promised to help me."

He pushed the now-empty plate away. "I'm sorry. I'm done. I got a whiff of this when I walked in and I couldn't say no."

Lucy nodded. "I understand, and I forgive you." She clapped her hands together. "But now it's time to get to work."

Emma laughed, and Marty rolled his eyes, standing from his seat.

"Lucy," Claire said slowly, "I heard you're planning to raise money? How?"

She was already walking away. "I'll show you!"

They followed her out of the tasting room, across the apple orchard and into the farm shop. It was closed to visitors, but it appeared Lucy had been hard at work. The displays were pushed away from the walls, some crowded into corners while others were rearranged and under a bright spotlight.

"What's going on in here?" Claire asked, admiring a shelf of neatly organized jams. Each jar had a strip of white ribbon tied elegantly around the top, and they were stacked in a perfect pyramid.

"Photoshoot. I decided to go with a new color scheme I found on Pinterest, too. It photographs better." Lucy walked behind the counter and spun a laptop around. "I started a GoFundMe page to raise money for the farm. So far, we've raised twenty thousand dollars! And that's just in a week!"

Claire pulled the screen closer. "Lucy! That's incredible! How did you do that?"

She spun the laptop back around and frowned. "I'm kind of disappointed, honestly."

Marty let out a laugh and Lucy turned her glare on him.

He quieted and pretended to zip his lips.

"So," Lucy said, "I made a couple of videos about the history of the farm, how it's changed, what we make – all that crap. People love it, they love a small town farm. It spread all over the internet and got picked up by a local news website on the mainland. That helped a lot."

Claire thought that was quite impressive. "How nice."

"It's not enough, though!" Lucy slammed the laptop shut and stood. "We need a lot more if we're going to make a dent at the auction."

"How much more?" Claire asked.

"At least thirty times that," Marty said quietly.

Claire took in a sharp breath. "Oh."

"Yeah, I know," Lucy said. "But Marty so kindly offered to help me update the website, and Emma is going to help me make more videos."

"Yes!" Emma said eagerly. "Anything you need!"

Marty picked up a wooden slingshot from a pile of children's toys, tugging and pretending to aim at the pyramid of glass jars. "What use are more videos?"

Lucy snapped the slingshot out of his hands. "For the Kickstarter we're making. And that is not a toy, Marty."

"Actually, it is," he countered. "A dangerous one. I'd like to buy one, please."

She tossed it back in the pile and turned to Claire. "Do you know what Kickstarter is?"

Claire shook her head. "Can't say I do."

"It's a fundraising tool, except it's a little different because when people donate, it makes them more like partners of the cause. At different levels of donation, they get a different reward. Say you donate ten dollars, and to thank you, I email you a picture of the farm to use as your phone background."

"No, of the goats!" Emma said. "I love the goats."

Lucy nodded, grabbing a notepad off the counter. "Pictures of goats..." she muttered, scribbling on the page. She then looked up. "The more they donate, the bigger the rewards. Maybe if someone donates fifty dollars, I'll send them a calendar of the farm. I don't know yet."

Claire suppressed a smile. This was just the sort of thing where Lucy excelled. She was creative – she took after her Aunt Becca in that way. "I think I get it. How can I help?"

Lucy flipped through her notebook, stopping at an entirely full page. "I was thinking that our top tier donors would get something even better. Maybe if they donate, like, five hundred dollars, they get a free night at the hotel?"

Claire shrugged. "Sure. No problem. That's easy."

Lucy clapped her hands together. "Yay! Perfect. I just came up with that five minutes ago. I want to meet with other business owners to see what we can come up with, but first I need to sit down and brainstorm – "

Marty interrupted her. "No, don't do that. If you stop moving, I'm pretty sure your brain will overheat."

Lucy rolled her eyes. "Ha, ha." She froze, then jolted a hand in the air. "Wait! I can also offer behind-the-scenes tours of the farm!"

"Not to be negative," Emma said in a small voice, "But won't that be hard to fulfill if the farm is sold off?"

Lucy stopped writing, scratching out the last thing she'd written. "Good point. We'll have Marty give a walking tour of Mount Constitution instead."

"Hey!" Marty set down the book he'd been flipping through about the history of Orcas Island. "I'll help, but you can't expect me to actually talk to people."

Claire stifled a laugh. "I'd pay to have Marty as a tour guide."

"Me too," Emma added.

He frowned and placed the book back on the shelf. "Let's get to talking about the website."

"Yes, let's!" Lucy pulled a second stool to the counter and took a seat in front of her computer.

Marty and Emma walked over, and as Claire took a step toward them, she was hit with a stabbing pain in her temple.

She stopped, taking a deep breath and putting a hand to her forehead.

Lucy, of course, noticed immediately. "Are you okay?"

Was that nausea? Or was she just too hot? Something was off, but she didn't want to worry Lucy. "I'm fine. I might be getting a migraine."

"Oh no!" Lucy stood, abandoning her computer. "Do you want me to drive you home?"

Claire waved a hand. "No, you're busy. I'm fine. I can get home."

"Let me drive you," Emma said. "I'll drop you off and then come back before Lucy even notices I'm gone."

A pulsating pain started behind her eye, then worsened when she looked up at the overhead lights in the shop. Yeah. Just a migraine. "If you don't mind, I would really appreciate it."

"Of course!" Emma picked up her purse. "I'll be back soon."

Lucy gave Claire a quick hug. "I'll check on you later."

Claire nodded. "Don't worry about me. Good luck, and let me know what I can do to help."

Before she walked out the door, Claire stopped and took one last look at Lucy. She was pointing at the computer screen, talking rapidly, as Marty listened and nodded his head.

As crazy as her plan sounded, it was nice to see Lucy energized again. Claire smiled to herself and followed Emma to her car.

Chapter Six

There was no word from Fiona, but Rob wasn't too concerned. He'd been busy most of the week taking meetings in Seattle, and he'd spent a lot of time at the Carriageway Holdings office. As far as he could tell, Fiona hadn't been in contact with them about his offer.

That was fine. They were in charge, not her. She seemed resigned to letting the farm go, though, which was the smart option. There wasn't much, if anything, she could do. It showed wisdom that she wasn't going to get stuck in a bitter fight to the end.

Carriageway Holdings, on the other hand, was not an organization that ran on wisdom. The people in charge were shrewd, impatient, and bitter. They had one goal – to make as much money as possible as quickly as possible.

Rob could work with that. He understood those sorts of people. They were, in some ways, his specialty.

At first, they didn't want to talk to him. They were in a hurry to bankrupt the farm and move on, giving him vague responses like "the financials for Grindstone just aren't adding up" and that their investors "needed to see a different type of progress."

With some digging, Rob figured out why Carriageway wasn't being forthcoming, and why they were dragging things out. Their sudden interest in bankruptcy wasn't a random occurrence – they were hard-pressed for cash and needed an infusion of funding for a new purchase: a large trailer park outside of Seattle.

It was an incredible investment. If Carriageway secured the property as their own, the sky would be the limit for profits. They could double the rents on day one, clear out all of the old residents and start anew. It was one of the hottest new trends in investing, and if Rob's company were able to get ahold of such a large rental community, they'd do the same thing.

They weren't quite at that level yet, though. Their investments were smaller and more calculated. They had to work harder and hustle more for new markets.

One day, they'd be one of the big players. Rob would make sure of it. He'd been with OSS for years, but he was only now being entrusted with a project of his own.

He was the one who had discovered Grindstone Farm, and he was leading the charge. This was his baby. He wasn't going to let the farm's failure go to waste.

The information about the trailer park proved to be invaluable. Once Rob knew what Carriageway was after, he was able to change his tactics. He talked to his boss and the lawyers at OSS to make sure the deal they gave Carriageway was better than whatever bankrupting the farm at auction could provide.

They were walking a fine line, but by Friday, it seemed like Carriageway was ready to get serious. There was a lot to prepare before he could strike up the formal deal with OSS's attorneys, not the least of which included Fiona's buy-in. Getting the farm staff on board would make things easier.

He flew back to Orcas Island that night and found his car waiting at the little airport just as he'd left it. It was odd being back on the quiet island after such a hectic week. He could see why some people liked the calm – for them it must be a sort of retreat.

Rob didn't need the calm. He had a busy weekend of work ahead of him, and that was just the way he liked it.

His first stop was the apartment he'd rented near East-sound. Despite being the lower level of a house, it felt secluded and private. It was small, but quiet – perfect for focusing on work.

Though he fully intended to get right down to business, he first peeked into the fridge. He opened the door and was disappointed to find nothing but a small wheel of cheese and half a pint of milk staring back at him.

Not ideal. Abandoning the apartment for a week would do that to a fridge, though, and he couldn't be at his most productive if he was hungry.

He decided to make the short trip into town to get dinner. He'd bring his work with him and go over some figures while having a sort of miniature celebration for himself. He'd never handled such a major deal on his own, and it was coming together perfectly. He deserved more than an old piece of cheese and questionable milk.

The first restaurant he walked into told him they were full for the night.

That was annoying, but he chalked it up to bad timing. He strolled into the place next door, only to get the same result.

He couldn't believe his bad luck. The restaurant didn't look like it was full, either.

"Can I take a seat at the bar?" he asked.

The hostess shrugged. "No. I'm sorry."

He started to wonder if the townspeople had a habit of shunning outsiders, but he was finally seated at the third restaurant he tried, a baroque-looking Asian fusion place.

Rob placed his order and settled in, spreading documents and folders around the table. It was a pleasant environment, cozy with peaceful music, and he could feel himself getting into the groove after finishing his first bowl of miso soup.

His peace was short-lived, however, broken by a familiar voice over his shoulder.

"Dinner for one?"

He turned to see Lucy standing behind him and he tucked the papers away before standing to greet her. "Guilty as charged. Unless you'd like to join me?"

"I would rather spend my evening digging oysters out of the mud," she said airily.

He wasn't sure what that meant, but it sounded like a no.

"We might be working together soon," he said.

"Actually, I don't think we'll be needing your services."

He raised an eyebrow. "Oh?"

She was trying to rattle him, but it wasn't going to work. Lucy had no idea what was coming. How could she? She was a nobody from an island in the middle of nowhere. She couldn't spot a multi-million-dollar deal if it were about to hit her in the face – which it was.

Lucy flashed a tight smile. "I just stopped by to talk to the owners of the restaurant. They're excited about a new partnership with the farm. I'm sure it's different in New York City, but in small towns like ours, relationships are important."

Rob motioned for her to take a seat. "Please, I'd love to learn more."

"No thanks."

"I'll buy you a drink."

She stopped, narrowed her eyes, and said, "Fine."

He suppressed a smile and flagged down the waitress. "I look forward to learning more about the community when I partner with Grindstone Farm."

Lucy shot him a positively disgusted look, but her face transformed into a smile when the waitress stopped by. "Hi, yes, I'd like a glass of plum wine, please. Thank you."

He forced himself to look at the drink menu so he wouldn't laugh. Lucy had no chance of making it in the business world. She wore all of her thoughts plainly on her face. Her disdain for him was so extreme that it was almost amusing.

She wasn't wrong to dislike him, of course. OSS had no intention of keeping Grindstone Farm together. The farm as it stood was basically worthless.

Maybe it was valuable to the community in some sentimental way, but it was worth much more in the hands of developers.

This was something Carriageway had missed in their haste. They assumed the farm could never pull in more than a quarter of a million dollars a year, and they were right. It couldn't make more than that. Not as a farm.

This was where Rob came in. Under his direction, OSS was in talks with a tech company in Silicon Valley called Grippy. They were going to build a brand-new compound on Orcas Island, offering high density housing, office space, and an idyllic company getaway for the up-and-coming startup.

All they needed was the farm's thirty acres. On a pristine location like Orcas Island, OSS could fetch upwards of six million dollars just for the land.

Lucy didn't know that, but at least she had the good sense to distrust him. Not that it would help her.

She spoke again. "You still don't look like you're dressed for farm work."

"I guess I need the right person to teach me." He took a sip of his beer. "Why do I feel like that might be you?"

She made a face, the disgust apparent once again. "Me? I'd rather send you into the pitch-black darkness of East Sound to dig up those oysters."

He wasn't going to let her comments get to him. He nodded placidly and said, "Sounds like a good start."

She ignored him and looked at the menu.

Rob took the opportunity to study her. She didn't look like a farmworker, either. Her clothing suggested she'd fit in on the streets of Seattle, but perhaps not in New York City. Though she had a definite sort of style, it was more of a West Coast chic. Less put together, less...try hard.

Her long red hair cascaded down her shoulders, and she was pretty, in a way. When she wasn't glaring at him.

He spoke again. "You seem strangely dedicated to that farm for someone who was moments away from handing in their notice."

Lucy's wine arrived and she accepted it with a thank you before turning to him. "That's all in the past."

"Were you planning to move to another farm? A competitor?"

She shook her head. "Of course not."

Interesting. "Is this the first farm you've worked for?"

"Maybe." She crossed her arms. "What does it matter?"

He smiled, keeping his tone light. "I'm curious, that's all. How long have you been at Grindstone?"

"How long have you been on Orcas Island?"

"About a week." He stared at her, waiting to see if she filled the silence. She did not. "How about you?"

"It doesn't matter how long I've been here. I know this island well. My mom owns a historic hotel overlooking the Sound – she saved it from destitution, actually. She's a pillar of the community."

"You're an expert, then?"

"Yes." Lucy leaned forward. "Just because I'm not wearing a two-thousand-dollar suit doesn't mean that I'm not competent, Mister ... whatever your name is."

He'd gotten under her skin. Rob forced himself not to smile. "Coolidge."

"Like the president?" She downed the rest of her small glass of wine.

"Sure. No relation, though."

She stared at him for a beat before adding, "Did you know Calvin Coolidge signed the Indian Citizenship Act?"

Rob wasn't sure where she was going with this, and he felt slightly embarrassed for not knowing anything about the former president who shared his surname. "I did not."

Lucy shrugged, her cool recovered. "Yep. 1925 – no, 1924. Just a bit of history for you. We're big on history here." She stood from her seat. "How lucky that you were able to get a table tonight. Enjoy the rest of your evening, and enjoy your trip back to New York."

Rob sat back. He felt like he'd been slapped in the face. It wasn't her disdain that had done it – that was nothing new for him, and she wasn't even particularly mean, compared to what he was used to.

What shocked him into silence was his own confusion after trying to keep up with her in conversation. He was pretty sure she'd insulted him, but he didn't understand how. And how did she know he had trouble getting a table?

She was something else.

He stared at her, unable to think of anything to say, and watched as she tossed her hair over her shoulder and walked out of the restaurant without looking back.

"Man," he muttered quietly, shaking his head and getting his papers back on the table.

It wasn't worth it to engage with her. He needed to focus on work.

Lucy was overflowing with confidence, though. Had she actually managed to find a better deal for the farm? Or was it just hubris?

It didn't matter. He knew what was going on. No one on Orcas Island was making decisions. Grindstone Farm was owned by Carriageway Holdings, and Rob was the only one who knew what they needed. He would finish this deal before Lucy knew what hit her.

Chapter Seven

It was wrong of her to taunt Rob. Lucy knew that, but she couldn't resist. His smug face had set her off. He thought he could just show up and take their farm, despite the fact that he knew nothing about farms, or Orcas Island, or even Calvin Coolidge!

Ha. Such a hotshot, except he could barely find a place to eat on the entire island. Lucy had personally made sure it would be difficult for him. She'd sent out an email to all of the restaurant owners she knew – well, that she and Claire knew – explaining what was happening to Grindstone and why Rob was terrible.

Almost all of the restaurant owners had responded enthusiastically about refusing to serve Rob, and they offered donations for the Kickstarter.

The *one* restaurant that hadn't responded to her email let Rob in. It was terrible luck, but Lucy talked to the owners – a couple in their sixties – and cleared everything up.

They weren't the most technology-focused people, so Lucy wasn't surprised they had missed her email. They were horrified when she told them about the prospect of Grindstone being sold off. They offered to add ten five-course meals to the growing list of Orcas Island experiences that Lucy had created for the Kickstarter campaign, which was extremely generous.

The list was getting long, and top donors would have a chance to do things like a personalized wine tasting at the winery, whale watching boat rides, and even a private helicopter tour above the islands.

The response from the community had been a bit overwhelming, to be honest. Islanders were so gracious and so willing to help. Lucy was in awe of how they pulled together, and the message was clear: Grindstone was not for sale.

Rob would eventually get the hint.

Still, she shouldn't taunt him. Lucy hadn't figured out all of the details quite yet. They were moving in the right direction – they'd just surpassed the two hundred-thousand-dollar mark for their fundraising – but that wasn't enough to buy the farm back at auction.

She had a feeling she was onto something big, though. Just the prior night, she'd gotten a sympathetic message from a local celebrity, Valerie Villano.

It was surely Margie's doing – she really knew everyone – and Lucy appreciated it. Valerie was a San Juan Island native turned 90's country pop star.

Sure, she wasn't as big as Taylor Swift, but she had been famous once! When Valerie had heard about Grindstone's plight, she'd asked Lucy if she could share information about the fundraising efforts on her Instagram page.

Lucy jumped at the idea, sending Valerie pictures and videos of the farm to use, and even offered to give her a private tour. Valerie said she was in LA, too far for a tour, but she promised to post something tomorrow morning.

Lucy couldn't wait. This could be just the boost they needed.

She was so excited that she stayed up until two o'clock in the morning editing a new video for the Kickstarter. She needed to get more footage of the island to show off how beautiful it was, but that would have to wait until the morning, and probably the next video...

After a refreshing four hours of sleep, she got back to work, and by the time Valerie made her post at ten, Lucy's new video was live and ready to go.

Within minutes, money started pouring in, along with words of support and encouragement.

Rob didn't have a chance.

By Monday, they crossed half a million dollars raised. People were going crazy for the curated Orcas Island experiences, and Valerie's promotion had launched them into the public eye.

Lucy couldn't believe it. First, she was happy, but that quickly grew to paranoia that someone would hack into her computer and steal all the money. After one sleepless night, she asked Marty for his help in making the account secure.

He walked her through setting strong passwords and gave her a stern lecture about not clicking on links she received in emails.

"You know what?" he finally said. "Just let me monitor your email for now. I don't mind, and I don't want you making any mistakes in your manic state."

Lucy laughed – or really, cackled, which only proved his point. She felt a little mad, but she liked that feeling. "Thanks, Marty." She paused. "You know, I don't care what people say about you. I like that you're a nerd."

He narrowed his eyes. "Thanks?"

Lucy had been keeping Fiona and the rest of the farm staff up to date on how the fundraising was going, and once they cracked the half a million mark, she came to Fiona with the plan.

"This is what you need to do," she said, storming into the trailer Monday morning. "Talk to your guy at Carriageway and convince him that no one is going to show up for a farm auction on a distant island. Make up whatever you need to – say that no one will want these farm supplies until the fall, because it's not the right time to plant apples, or something."

Fiona made a face. "They don't need to plant apples right away to – "

"Yes but *they* don't know that. Just make it convincing. Then tell them how much money I've raised, and tell them that I'll be at the auction to buy everything anyway."

Fiona bit her lip. "What if you can't get everything? What if someone else outbids you and the farm is still split up?"

"I haven't gotten there yet, but we'll figure something out."

"I don't know, Lucy." Fiona sunk into her desk. "I've been talking to Rob, and he thinks – "

"Do not talk to Rob! He's the enemy!" Lucy stopped and cleared her throat. "I'm sorry. I didn't mean to yell."

Fiona was unfazed. She only laughed; her cheer had been coming back more and more these days. "He's not so bad, you know. He's been explaining things to me."

Lucy rolled her eyes. "Really? Did he explain how he's going to make money off the farm?"

"Sort of. I think I get it."

She couldn't let Rob get to Fiona. "No, listen to me. We have the entire county behind us. People are rooting for us! They want the farm to stay. We'll beat this bankruptcy, okay?"

Fiona took a deep breath and smiled. "Okay."

"So you'll talk to Carriageway?"

"Sure," she said with a shrug. "I'll do my best."

Lucy stood and leaned forward. "Maybe I should talk to them, too?"

Fiona's "no" came a little too quickly. Lucy frowned.

Fiona rushed to speak again. "Leave the farm talk to me, okay?"

Fair enough. "Okay, fine. But let me know what they say."

Chapter Eight

The migraine had only been the start of Claire's problems. It ruined the weekend and her plans with Chip, much to Chip's disappointment. He tried to hide it, but Claire could tell he was down about having to do the pairing tasting on his own.

He didn't stay down long, though, and planned a romantic dinner for two on the mainland the following Friday. Claire was excited for it, but at work on Monday, she started feeling off again.

At first, she thought it might be another migraine, so against her normal routine, she forced herself to take a preemptive nap. The migraine never came, but nausea and other unpleasant symptoms rolled in on Wednesday.

By Thursday, her situation had grown worse, or as Chip put it, "explosive." She had to cancel their plans again, and he assured her he was happy to spend the weekend playing nurse.

Claire felt horribly guilty. Not only had she repeatedly ruined Chip's attempts at being romantic, but then he had to pick up her responsibilities at the hotel, too. She insisted that she could care for herself and that he needed to stay away so he wouldn't get sick, but he wouldn't hear it. He was at her house day and night, ready with drinks, popsicles, broth and crackers.

Between delirious bouts of sleep where she disappeared from the world, he also apparently doused her bathroom in bleach, leaving it a sparkling clean palace for her to run into.

By Monday, she was more or less functional again and insisted he return to work. The next day, she felt strong enough to show up at The Grand Madrona herself.

At first, she felt okay. She'd had a burst of energy in the morning that fooled her into thinking she was better. At lunch time, though, she started to struggle. Margie called to chat and Claire could barely focus on the conversation.

Unfortunately for Claire, Margie noticed. "Do you remember her music?"

Claire took a sip of water before answering. "I'm sorry, whose music?"

"Valerie Villano! I know country isn't your style, but she's a San Juan Island girl. I met her last summer and..."

Claire stood from her desk and the room started spinning. She dropped her phone, trying to steady herself on a nearby wall.

She could still hear Margie chattering away, but when she stooped to pick up the phone, she somehow slammed her head into the desk.

"What was that?" Margie's voice blared through the phone, loud and clear.

"Nothing," Claire said. "Just dropped the phone. Hang on, I need to find it..."

When she finally fumbled it back into her hands, Margie was gone. Claire assumed they'd been disconnected, but moments later, Chip burst into the office.

"Claire, are you okay? Margie just called me, she said you weren't making sense and – "

"No, it's nothing." Claire had just struggled her way back into her chair. "Don't overreact. I just need a little nap. I dropped the phone, that's all."

"You're bleeding."

"What?" She reached a hand up to her forehead and felt a sharp pain. Her hand was covered in blood. "That's not good."

"I'm taking you to the hospital."

"I don't have time to go to the hospital!" Claire said, trying to sound firm, but her voice only sounded high and weak.

He knelt down so they were eye to eye. His voice was gentle. "Honey, at the very least, you need stitches. Let's just see what the doctor thinks, okay?"

Claire let out a sigh. Stitches shouldn't take long, at least. "Fine."

She stood, and Chip helped steady her. Somehow, with him around, she felt dizzier. She told herself it was probably from him fussing too much, though it concerned her that she needed his help all the way to the car.

Chapter Nine

Lucy got a call from Chip on her drive home from Grindstone. She answered on Bluetooth and loudly yelled, "What's up, dude?"

"Hey Lucy. Are you busy?"

She frowned. Generally, she could count on a jovial response from him, or at least a bit of teasing. He didn't sound right. "Just driving. Why?"

"I don't want you to panic," he said.

Lucy immediately felt fear building in her chest. "What happened?"

"Nothing bad. Are you in the car? Maybe you should pull over."

"Just spit it out!"

"Well, you know Claire had that stomach bug," he said, voice low and solemn.

"Yeah? Is she okay?"

"She's fine," he said. "She said you would panic."

"Well, when you're this bad at relaying information, yes, I am going to panic. But she's fine?"

"She fell and hit her head. She needed some stitches," he said.

"Oh." Lucy took a deep breath. Her face felt tingly, and that usually happened when she forgot to breathe. "Just some stitches. Okay."

He was quiet for a moment. "The doctor was worried about how dizzy she was. She wants her to get checked out, just to make sure it's not something more serious."

"More serious like what?" Lucy spotted a gas station ahead and turned on her blinker to pull in. It was too hard to drive and think at the same time.

"They don't have the machines they need here for testing, though, so they sent her to the mainland."

She pulled into a spot and put her car into park. "Okay, that makes sense. What do they think could be wrong?"

"Uh, what they said is – it might be a stroke."

Lucy's entire body went numb. "Claire had a *stroke?*"

"They don't know yet," he said quickly. "That's what they're going to find out. She feels okay, though. She's still talking and arguing with me – "

"Can I talk to her?"

"Not right now. She's being transported. They're flying her over."

Flying her over!

It was getting impossible to breathe. Lucy punched at her car door, trying to open the window.

"Don't panic, though, okay?" Chip's voice was low and calm. "It's just a concern. Claire thinks it's all silly, but she agreed to go."

"She downplays *everything*. You can't listen to her!" The window finally opened. It didn't help much, but it was something. "Where is she going? I'll meet you there."

"Just hang tight, and I can update you when – "

"No. I'll get on the ferry now, or I'll swim if I have to. Where is she going?"

"Bellingham."

"Got it." Lucy took a deep breath. "I'm going to leave now. Send me the hospital name."

"All right. I'm almost there. I'll see you soon."

She accidentally hung up on him before saying goodbye. Oh well, Chip would forgive her.

She pulled up the ferry schedule and saw that if she hurried, she could make the next sailing.

In some strange time warp, only seconds later she pulled her car onto the ferry. As they set off, she took a moment to catch her breath.

Searching online for symptoms of strokes wasn't helpful. He said Claire was still arguing with him, so that was good, right? That was a good sign, if she could talk?

Her frantic search was interrupted when a call from Fiona popped up on her screen. She dismissed it. There was no time to talk to anyone.

Yet she probably needed to tell everyone else what was going on. Chip had done a terrible job. She'd keep it simple. She pulled up her group text with Marty, Lillian, and Rose and typed out a message.

"Chip just called. Claire isn't feeling well. Needed stitches for some reason? I guess she fell. Doctor thought she might be having a stroke. Being flown to the mainland now. I'm on my way. I'll let you know what else I find out."

There. That was the way to do it.

She tucked her phone away and returned to her car. Time had continued at warp speed, and the ferry would soon dock in Anacortes.

Lucy could keep it together as long as she had some sort of tangible task in front of her. Right now, it was driving to that hospital. Her GPS said it was an hour away.

Surely it wouldn't take that long.

Chapter Ten

Carriageway was basically in the bag and Rob was on cloud nine. He'd known it would work out in the end, but the chase was always tense.

Still, Rob enjoyed everything about the chase – the push and pull, the charm, the outwitting and outsmarting. A rockier course meant a more satisfying reward, and this had been the biggest deal of his career. It would set him up not just at OSS, but for life.

Carriageway was having their lawyers look over the paperwork now, and if all went well, the deal would be signed by the end of the week.

The end of the *week!*

Rob was on top of the world. If only he could see Lucy's face when she found out...

Oh well. Can't have everything. He decided to use his spare time to go the extra mile for their future partner: driving around the island and making note of the different amenities Grippy could talk up to their employees.

There wouldn't be as much as they were used to in Silicon Valley, so Rob needed to play up the rugged, peaceful aspect of Orcas. That's what they were coming for, right?

Of course, that's what they'd say, but they wouldn't mean it. They wanted to feel like they were somewhere different without sacrificing anything. The fact that there wasn't a single Starbucks on the island could start a riot. They wanted remote, but still entirely connected. Distant, yet not inconvenienced.

That was impossible, of course, but Rob was happy to play along with the fantasy. Maybe some things could be built into the Grippy campus to make them feel more at home – yoga studios, or restaurants that rotated cuisines. The island had a variety of places to eat – not that Rob could ever get a table – but it wouldn't be enough to keep the Grippy staff happy.

Not only were there no Starbucks, but there were not enough coffee shops in general. Grippy had over a thousand employees. How many would flood onto the island? Five hundred? A thousand, if they brought their families?

That was a lot of coffees. The island had a population of under five thousand right now, and an influx of people might make things tight, but that wasn't his problem. His role was to deliver the land Grippy needed, something no other company had managed to do before.

Rob could see why it had taken so long. The island wasn't open to development. There were a lot of family farms, little homes, and sentimental small business.

It had charm, sure, but it wasn't maximized for profit. It was maximized for something else, something intangible and irrelevant, really.

It took him a few hours to explore and comb through the west side of the island. He hoped the east side would go more quickly, but he was sorely mistaken.

He was first slowed down by the state park. The main road went right through it, forcing him to slow down behind bikers and hikers and other people who should have been at work.

This could potentially be sold as slowing down to enjoy the views. Not that Rob ever had time to enjoy views, and he didn't expect the people at Grippy did, either.

It was a nice idea, but in any real business, slowing down was a fantasy. Maybe that's what this compound would be? A great fantasy surrounded by the sea.

Once he got past the park, he drove around the town of Olga, looping along the bottom of the island and then back north.

The properties here had a fascinating variability. There were a few businesses on this side of the island, ranging from high-end restaurants to low-key eateries.

Most interestingly, interspersed between expensive restaurants and art galleries were properties that looked like complete and total dumps. There could be a multimillion-dollar house butting up to four acres of overgrown grass with a rundown trailer plopped in the middle.

Some of the homes looked like they hadn't been updated in decades, others looked completely abandoned. Then, only a hundred feet down the road, would stand a verifiable compound with an ocean view.

It boggled the mind. Why hadn't all of this been bought up already? Why hadn't it all been developed?

There were luxury offerings. One of the tour companies had a gorgeous, pirate-looking ship which hosted sunset cruises and wildlife watching. Surely that'd be a favorite? The Grippy employees might even like the park – paddle boarding or hiking, whatever it was they did with their little free time.

He was nearly through his east side tour when he got a call from his boss.

Rob smiled as he answered. He was probably calling to congratulate him. "Hey Rick. Good to hear from you."

"Is it?" His voice boomed through the car's speakers. "Even though you blew it?"

"Whoa, whoa. Blew what?"

"Carriageway. They're done."

Rob rolled his eyes. Rick was a jumpy guy. "They're looking the deal over. Don't scare them off. The plan is to sign at the end of the week and – "

"They just filed for bankruptcy. Does that sound like a company that's ready to make a deal with you?"

Rob's breath caught in his throat. "What?"

"Oh, now you're surprised? Thanks for catching up."

"This has to be a mistake," Rob said.

"Yeah, your mistake! I thought you were on top of this. Why did I send you out there if I wind up knowing about things before you do?"

Rob was used to being yelled at, but sometimes it was impossible to get through to Rick when he was in a mood. "All right, this will be fine. If they're filing for bankruptcy, we'll just buy the land at auction. It might go up a bit, but we can – "

"They filed for Chapter 11, you idiot. Do you know what that means?"

Rob's heart sank. Of course he knew what it meant. It meant he'd failed, and he was probably going to get fired.

Rick continued. "Yeah. That's right. They're keeping the land, and auctioning the rest of the crap. Completely useless to us."

Rob might have been a failure, but he was still a quick thinker. "I'll find a new location for the developers."

"Oh yeah, just find a new one, he says." Rick kicked something and loudly swore. "Like we haven't thought of that before. You've lost us millions on this deal."

"I've got an idea."

Rick's voice had dropped to an almost comical snarl. "It had better be a good one."

"What was that hotel we were looking at initially? On the island?"

Rick paused. "It was called The Madrona Grand, or something."

"That one!" Rob said.

"That's not going to work. The owners wouldn't sell, and it wasn't worth the hassle to chase them out when Grindstone was circling the drain."

Rob slowed down as he pulled onto The Grand Madrona Hotel's long driveway. The hotel stood tall, beautiful and proud, with the ocean sparkling behind it.

Rob took a deep breath. "I have a plan. Let me work this."

Chapter Eleven

After four days in the hospital, one CT scan, two MRIs, and countless tiny cans of ginger ale, Claire was cleared to go home. Her final diagnosis?

Dehydration.

Lucy was shocked when she heard it, so much so that she spent fifteen minutes interrogating the first man who wandered into Claire's room wearing a white coat.

She'd assumed he was the head neurologist. However, it turned out he was the physician's assistant for the family medicine group.

Apparently, Lucy had missed the attending neurologist because she was a young-looking woman with pretty, cascading curls and muted blue scrubs.

Lucy was embarrassed by her sexism, but she didn't let shame hold her back long. Once she realized her mistake, she cornered the pretty Dr. Baker and resumed her interrogation right where she'd left off.

The doctor was kind, and probably overly patient, but no matter how much Lucy pressed, she wouldn't admit Claire was in danger.

"Don't you think she should stay a bit longer? Another week or two?" Lucy asked.

Up close, Dr. Baker looked older and wiser than Lucy initially realized. She also had kind eyes and a warm smile. "No, that's not necessary. We've ruled out any neurological causes and your mom is okay to go home. She can follow up and..."

Lucy stopped listening after hearing "no." She didn't mean to, but from the first moment she'd seen Claire in that hospital bed, she knew something was terribly wrong.

Yes, Claire was smiling and calm and normal looking, but that was exactly how Claire would go out – with a smile on her face while assuring everyone she was okay.

Lucy couldn't let that happen. Someone had to stand up for her! But despite her pushing and questioning, Claire was discharged on Sunday, and everyone acted like it was great news.

Both Lillian and Rose had rushed to the hospital after getting Lucy's panicked texts. Now that Claire was allegedly healthy, they both thought it was funny to tease Lucy about how scared she'd gotten.

Lucy refused to accept any criticism, jokingly or not. "Next time someone is having a stroke, I'll make sure my first thought is to remember to be cool about it."

Rose snorted a laugh, but Lillian was more sympathetic. "I know you worry," she said, "but I truly think Mom is okay."

After Claire left the hospital with Chip to get lunch in Bellingham, the rest of them walked out to the parking lot, a gray sky hanging above like an omen. Would it rain? Would it hold? Would Claire make it back to the island or have to be airlifted off the island again?

There was no way to tell. Lucy let out a sigh. "We'll see. Do either of you want a ride to Orcas Island? My apartment has a second bedroom. You're welcome to stay."

"I wish I could," Rose said. "I only have one more day off work for the rest of the year, so I need to get back home. I'm going to try to catch a flight tonight."

Lucy shrugged. "Next time."

Lillian broke into a smile. "I can come. My job is fully remote now, so I don't have to rush home."

Though Lucy would love nothing more than to have a guest, Lillian had a long-term boyfriend back in Texas. "What about Mason? Won't he miss you?"

"He'll be okay on his own for a while," Lillian said. "He's traveling for work right now, so he won't even notice."

Good enough. "Okay, great!"

Marty stopped by Lucy's car, a book bag slung over his shoulder. "Anyone headed to the airport?"

"I am," Rose said.

"Marty." Lucy shuddered. "I can't believe you're going to fly back to Orcas when there's a perfectly good ferry an hour's drive away."

He nodded solemnly. "You're right. It'd be better if it took three times as long and involved both a car and a boat."

"Well, don't you just know everything," Lucy snapped. "Not just the best way to travel, but that Claire didn't have a stroke – "

"They know Mom didn't have a stroke because they checked *multiple* times," Lillian said gently.

"Why are you so stuck on the stroke thing?" Rose asked. "They gave us good news. There was no stroke. Why can't you accept it?"

"*Because*," Lucy hissed, "they never should have used the word 'stroke' if they didn't know what they were talking about. You can't just put 'stroke' into people's heads and expect it to go away!"

"That's true," Marty added. "You can't put a stroke into someone's head and then take it away."

Lillian and Rose laughed.

Lucy gritted her teeth. It was fine if they wanted to joke around, but Lucy knew she should have kept a closer eye on Claire. This had all happened when she was distracted. From now on, she wouldn't let herself get caught up in things that didn't matter, like farms, and men with expensive suits.

Lucy got into her car. "Enjoy your flights. I truly hope you don't crash and die."

Marty nodded. "Always a comfort when you say that, Lucy."

"I know!" She smiled and shut the car door.

Lucy had only been on a plane twice in her life. Though it was on the advice of her therapist, both times felt like she was going to die, and she promised herself she would never undergo that turmoil again. A plane crash had already killed her parents. How could anyone be sure a plane wouldn't try to kill her, too?

Marty was wrong about the ferry. Their trip back was lovely, and Lillian gushed over the views. Lucy had a hard time focusing on how nice they were, but she was glad Lillian was enjoying herself. She was still in her own world, jarred from it only when she got a call from Aunt Becca.

"I heard Claire's doing better," Becca said. "I'm glad."

"I guess." Lucy stood up and dropped her voice. "I'm not convinced."

Becca grunted. "Me either. You should keep an eye on Claire."

"I think so too!" Lucy shot a look at Lillian, who was still engrossed with the view of the passing islands. "Everyone else thinks I'm just crazy."

"You're not crazy. You care, which sometimes can look like crazy."

Dang, Aunt Becca dropping in the wisdom. "Yeah."

"I'll be out to visit again soon. I miss seeing you guys."

"We miss you too!"

"Marty's been talking to me," Becca said with a laugh. "Can you believe it? We talk almost every week."

It had taken him long enough. "That's nice, Aunt B. We'll get together when you visit, okay?"

"Sure thing. Take care of Claire for me."

"I will."

Thankfully, Lillian had missed the entirety of that conversation, and they soon arrived at the Orcas Island ferry terminal. After getting Lillian settled, Lucy drove straight to Claire's house with the intent of helping her settle in, only to be shooed away.

"Lucy, I'm fine," Claire insisted. "The only thing I need is a good night's sleep. That's one thing you can't get at a hospital."

"How about I stay here with you in case you don't feel well and need someone to call the air ambulance again?"

Claire shook her head. "You need to get back to your life! And the farm. Margie told me they're close to raising six hundred thousand dollars now? You've done an amazing job!"

Huh. Lucy hadn't checked on the fundraisers in days. "Thanks."

Lillian turned to her, eyes wide. "I'm sorry. How much money did you raise?"

"I'll tell you later," Lucy said, waving a hand. "We'll let Claire get some rest."

Lucy took Lillian out to dinner in town and explained the situation at the farm.

"It was so important to me to rescue the farm," she said, "but now I kind of don't care anymore."

That made Lillian laugh. "Oh come on, Lucy. How can you leave them hanging now? You at least have to help with this auction. When is it?"

She bit her lip. "I don't know, but I can find out. I'll talk to Fiona tomorrow. Maybe I could just give her the money and let her handle it."

"But then what're you going to do with all that free time and nervous energy?"

Lucy stared at her glass of water. Good question. She hadn't had time to think about that. "I don't know. It seems like my work here is done."

"Why don't you see where it goes?"

Lucy rolled her eyes. "Fine. But I'm not going to get all wrapped up in it again and miss out on everything important."

Lillian stared at her and nodded slowly. "Okay. No one is asking you to."

After catching up with Lillian and a night of decent sleep, Lucy had the strength to face Fiona in the morning.

What she lacked in enthusiasm Fiona more than made up for.

"I can't believe they went for it!" Fiona said, pacing the length of the trailer.

"For bankruptcy?" Lucy nodded. "It's the easy way out."

"It is, and we found a way for us to keep the land, so all we need to get back at auction is our equipment. You know, from the distillery, the apple picker, the freezers..."

Lucy stared at the auction list in front of her. Who would want all this crap? "When is the auction?"

"Three weeks from now. I don't know how we're going to do it. Anyone could show up and outbid us."

"Can't we just buy new stuff?" Lucy asked.

"We'd need more than double the money you've raised to buy everything new."

Lucy made a face. "Sheesh. Why is farming so expensive?"

Fiona laughed. "That's the business. Are you sure you're okay? You seem down."

"I'm just a little tired. Don't worry. I'm fine."

"Good." She paused. "I'm a little worried about Rob."

"Oh?" A smile crept over Lucy's face. "Was he upset?"

Fiona started to speak, then stopped herself.

"Tell me!" Lucy said, leaning forward.

"Well, no, not upset. He was very nice about it all. Which made me worried that his company might still plan to snap everything up. They could, you know. I never really understood what he wanted from us."

"That's a good point. He's still dangerous." Lucy drummed her fingers on the table before shooting up from her seat. "I'm going to find him. Do you know where his office is? I'll get it out of him."

"Do you really think he'll tell you? I didn't get the impression that the two of you got along."

"I can be *extremely* charming," Lucy said. "Now hand over the address."

Fiona didn't protest, hiding her smile as she wrote the address down on a scrap of paper.

Lucy snapped it from her hand. "I'll talk to you soon!"

She turned and walked through the door, speed-walking to her car. It turned out there was still some fun to be had.

Chapter Twelve

When Rob had rented a small second floor office on the island, he'd had no way of knowing how awful it would be. If he'd had the time to stop by and check it out in person, he would've noticed the flaws, but time was money and he had excess of neither.

Because of that, he was now subjected to the smell of fried fish from the next-door restaurant ten hours a day. He thought that would be the worst of it, but then the fitness studio directly beneath him resumed their classes after a winter break.

There was a high-energy spin class every day, complete with pulsing music and an instructor that yelled encouragements over a microphone. On top of that, the twice daily dance classes had a thirty-minute stretch where participants seemingly took turns kicking the walls and jumping into the ceiling.

It was impossible to focus, and infuriatingly, Rob couldn't figure out how to get his new idea to work.

It was a long shot, but he *needed* it to work. Plus, as far as he was concerned, The Grand Madrona Hotel was a far better site for Grippy's compound. It had stunning ocean views, it was minutes from that stupid state park, and there was under-developed land all around it.

The new owner had underpaid for it, because until recently, the old hotel had been struggling. A few months ago, Rick tried scaring the owner into selling, but she hadn't taken the bait.

Why would she? Business was booming now, from what Rob could tell.

He knew there must be a way in. He just needed to find it. If he didn't, he'd be fired, and it'd be next to impossible to get another job with his failure trailing behind him. He'd be a has-been, an unemployable joke.

Rob had promised to have his plan to Rick within a couple of days, and so far, he'd come up with exactly nothing. The hotel was untouchable. No noise complaints, no code violations, and hardly any bad reviews.

Surely the owner had to be doing *something* wrong? Tax evasion? Laundering money? Hiding drug lords in the penthouse suite?

Whatever it was, he was determined to find it and exploit it.

He was lost in a stack of paperwork when there was a knock on the door to his office.

At first, he didn't hear it. His ears were filled with the spinning instructor imploring his students to "reach deep inside for the strength to power on!"

The door creaked open and he jumped in surprise. No one had come to see him before.

"Hello?" called out a voice.

He covered up the papers on his desk before responding. "Come on in!"

Rob stood, hoping that by some miracle an answer to his problems would walk through the door.

It ended up just being Lucy.

"Interesting office you've got yourself," she said.

"Thanks. I'd offer you a set of earplugs, but I'm fresh out."

"I appreciate the consideration, but I'm here to talk to you and earplugs might make that difficult."

Rob motioned for her to take a seat. There was only one other chair in the embarrassingly empty office. He couldn't even offer her coffee. "You're here to talk? Or to gloat?"

She sat down, smiling warmly. "Rob, I would *never* gloat. I'm not a sore winner. I hope we can still be friends."

"Friends?" He smiled back at her. Her being here made the office look like an empty jail, and that she was here to be interrogated. Or maybe he was the one who'd be interrogated? "Of course. I don't hold a grudge."

Her eyes narrowed ever so slightly. "Why not?"

"It's not my style."

"I don't believe you."

He wasn't entirely benevolent in his forgiveness, and he was happy to tell her why. "Grudges aren't useful. Besides, you know the area better than I do. If we stay friends, you might help me."

She frowned. "Aren't you leaving?"

"No, not yet."

"Oh." She sat back.

"You seem disappointed."

She let out a breath and smiled again. "No, just a little surprised, I guess."

Rob sat back and crossed his arms. What did she care that he was still here? He wasn't going to go after the farm. She'd won that battle, somehow. Maybe she'd bribed them.

No. He knew it was his own fault. He'd misjudged Carriageway's needs.

Either way, the farm was useless to him now. "You've won. I'm not going to fight with you."

"Not even for our top-of-the-line distillery technology?"

That made him laugh. "I have no idea what to do with those sorts of things, as you well know. I still haven't mucked out a stall, and to be honest, I'm relieved I won't have to."

She just stared at him.

He met her silence with his own silence.

Finally, she said, "So what do you want?"

"I'm not sure." He got up, turning to look out of the small window behind his desk before facing her again. "My boss is pretty unhappy with me, as you can imagine."

She made a face, almost like a wince, before quickly recovering. "That stinks. You could always quit."

"Hm." The thought had never even crossed his mind. "Not yet. I'd like to still find something on the island. Some business to revive."

"That's what you want? To revive something?"

He nodded. "It is. Maybe you could help me. I'm getting nowhere on my own. I don't know anyone and I can't even get a table for dinner around here."

"Oh, that was because of me." She flashed a grin. "I told everyone I knew not to serve you."

"Really?" He stared at her, at a loss for words. "How incredibly..."

She cut him off. "Petty?"

"No." He shook his head. "Brilliant. It worked well. You must know a lot of people."

Lucy smiled. "I do."

"Will you help me? I'm just trying not to get fired."

She sat back, studying him for a moment. "Only if you promise to stay away from Grindstone."

He stuck a hand out. "Sure. Let's make a deal."

She kept her arms firmly crossed. "If I see you anywhere near that auction, you go right back on the do-not-serve list. I might get you banned from the ferry, too."

He didn't know how she would do it, but he believed she was capable of it. "I won't try to buy anything at the auction, I swear. Actually, if you want, I can talk you through it. I've been to a few auctions."

"Fine." She paused. "I mean, deal. I guess."

They shook hands.

Maybe she could help him, or maybe not, but at least he'd be able to get a decent meal for once.

Chapter Thirteen

That was enough acting chummy. Lucy stood from her seat. "I'd better get back to work. There's a lot to prepare."

"Maybe we could get together for dinner today and I could try to help?" he asked.

Ha. Dinner.

She shouldn't have told him about her glorious scheme to keep him out of the island's restaurants. It was some of her finest work.

That was her problem. Well, one of her many problems. Lucy didn't have a poker face, and he looked so pathetic in that empty office. As soon as she felt guilt creeping in about what she'd done, she blabbed.

"We can meet at the fish and chip shop next door," she offered. "How's five?"

"That works. Just out of curiosity, did you happen to tell them to vent their fryer exhaust directly into my office?"

"Nope. They're doing that all on their own."

"Terrific."

"See you later." Lucy turned and walked out. She had no interest in becoming friends with this guy. He was sleazy. Up to no good. She could just feel it in her bones.

It was just like how she knew Claire was sick. She trusted her intuition, even if everyone else thought she was being ridiculous.

Aunt Becca didn't think she was ridiculous! But then again, everyone thought Aunt Becca was ridiculous too, or at best, eccentric...

Whatever.

They could think whatever they wanted to think of her. Lucy knew what she was about. She would keep her friends close, and keep Rob closer.

She went back to the farm and spent the day researching auctions, but didn't get terribly far. There wasn't a wealth of information on how to keep people from showing up and legally stealing their farm equipment.

Most of her ideas to keep auction attendees away were frowned upon, if not fully illegal. For example, she wasn't allowed to threaten people, she couldn't lie about the quality of the equipment – well, she could try, but who would believe her? And she *definitely* wasn't supposed to advertise a different date for the auction so people missed it.

After hours of scheming, Lucy had nothing. When it was time to meet with Rob again, she felt like the wind had been taken out of her sails.

He, on the other hand, was as chipper as ever. "What's good here?"

"I don't know, actually," she said. "We don't have to eat here. I thought it was a good place to meet."

"Did you suggest meeting so I didn't have an excuse to ask for your phone number?"

Rude. Of course she hadn't wanted to give him her phone number. She wanted as little to do with him as possible while still having complete control over the situation. "No," she lied, "that wasn't it."

"Because rest assured," he said, looking up at the menu on the wall, "you're not my type."

Lucy threw a hand to her chest. "Oh Rob, you have to stop breaking my heart like this."

He looked back at her, smiling. "I just mean I don't pursue women through work, so you don't have to worry about any unwanted advances. It's unprofessional."

Right. She was probably too smart for him. Or too annoying. She'd gotten that feedback from more than one guy.

Lucy knew she just scared them. "Correct. Very unprofessional."

A man in an apron came to the counter, sweat pooling on the tip of his nose, just about to drop off. "What can I get you?"

Lucy glanced at the menu, then back at him. He really must've been slaving over that fryer. "I'd like the fried cod, please."

"You want the fries and drink combo?"

"Definitely."

He looked at Rob. "How about you?"

"I'll take the salmon burger with a side salad."

The man punched their orders into the register, and Lucy was disappointed the sweat drop had fallen off of his nose without her seeing where it went.

In the meantime, Rob had pulled out his wallet and handed over his credit card.

"I'll pay for myself," Lucy said, digging a twenty dollar bill out of the bottom of her purse.

The guy nodded, took their payments, and left.

Lucy turned to Rob. "I can't help but notice how annoyingly healthy your meal choice was."

"I don't eat a lot of fried foods," he said. "It messes with my system."

She rolled her eyes. Probably watching his figure. "I didn't realize you were so finely tuned."

He laughed, motioning toward a table near the window. "I'm not. It just makes me sick. I have what you might call a sensitive stomach."

Oh. "That's too bad." The entirety of her meal would come out of a fryer, and she couldn't wait.

They sat down and Lucy, tired of thinking about the farm, decided to see how much information she could pry out of Rob. "What's your story, Mr. Sensitive Stomach? Where are you from?"

"I was born and raised in New York City."

"A city boy." That tracked. "Is that why you're so intense?"

A laugh burst out of him. "*I'm* intense?"

She nodded. "You've been working in a hot office next to a seafood joint for the last, I don't know, twelve hours? And you're still wearing a suit."

He glanced down as if to confirm what he was wearing, then looked back up at her. "I like suits."

"Why?" She leaned in. "Did your dad wear a suit to work every day?"

"He did." Rob took a sip of his water. "I don't think that's the reason, though."

She crossed her arms. "Maybe, maybe not. What does he do?"

"He's a hedge fund manager at one of the biggest companies in New York."

Interesting. "So you're following in his footsteps."

"Not really. My dad was a lot more successful by the time he was my age."

"How old are you?"

He leaned in. "How old are *you?*"

"Thirty-four," she said without missing a beat. She didn't care to subscribe to the fear of her age increasing. She'd earned each and every one of those years.

A slight smile danced on his lips. "I'm a year older than you, and at my age, my dad was already a partner."

"That was what, the eighties? Things are different now."

"My dad doesn't take that as an excuse. He expects all of his kids to achieve great things."

Yikes. Claire had never put pressure on them like that. She just wanted them to be happy. "How's that going?"

Rob shrugged. "Not bad. My younger brother started a tech company in Silicon Valley; they're about to go public. And my older brother...well, he's the black sheep of the family."

Lucy had to stop herself from suggesting he was the only normal one. Instead, she said, "Let me guess. You had all of the best tutors, went to the best schools, and played all the best sports?"

A ding rang out and two red baskets appeared on the counter.

"Something like that," he said before popping up to grab their food. "It was a good way to grow up, and I don't want to waste it."

She made a face before she could stop herself. "Waste it how?"

"By being a failure."

"A failure at what, though?"

"Life."

Oh man. This guy was too much. Here he was, probably sitting on an MBA from an Ivy League school, determined to "win" at life.

He was an even simpler rival than she'd realized. He had no idea what he was doing.

Lucy smiled. Maybe he wasn't *so* dangerous.

Chapter Fourteen

The salmon burger was better than Rob had hoped, and Lucy's interrogation carried on about as intensely as he'd expected.

Rob didn't mind doing all of the talking, but he was curious about Lucy's background. He decided to tread carefully, though, because prickly Lucy tended to shut down rather abruptly.

"Is this your first farm auction?" he asked when she took a break from pelting him with questions to take a sip of her soda.

"Yes."

"And your first farm job?"

She set the empty glass down. "Yes. Why?"

Already defensive. "Just wondering. I've been to three farm auctions, but I've never worked on a farm."

"I've worked a lot of places," she said. It seemed like she wanted to say more, but she had stopped herself.

"Oh?"

Lucy stuffed a handful of fries into her mouth before responding. "I like variety."

He nodded. "I can see that."

Lucy cleared her throat. "So what am I supposed to do to keep people from showing up and buying our equipment?"

The salad hadn't been a bad choice, but those fries looked a lot more enticing. He'd been nauseous all day yesterday though, and didn't need to tempt fate...

"You can't stop anyone from showing up. The best you can do is strategize. You know, figure out what you can afford to lose and what you can't."

"We can't afford to lose anything," she said.

"I don't believe you."

She narrowed her eyes. "It's a family farm, Rob, not an investment bank."

"Yet you raised over half a million dollars like it was nothing. You're telling me you can't afford to lose an apple picker?"

"No. We can't."

So much for being reasonable. "Where's the auction list?"

"I'm not showing you that."

He had to stop himself from rolling his eyes. "It's public knowledge. I can go home and look at it."

"Does that mean you haven't looked at it yet?"

He shook his head. "No. I told you, I'm not interested in that stuff."

She eyed him for a moment before leaning down and pulling a paper from her purse. She unfolded it to reveal a short list with handwritten notes in the margins.

"Don't read that," she said, covering the left corner with her hand.

She still didn't trust him. That was fine. He didn't need her trust. He needed her help.

He leaned forward and studied the list. They weren't auctioning the land, which was nothing short of a miracle. If the land were up for grabs, it would've turned into a wild bidding war between developers and hedge funds. That would've been ugly.

The rest of this stuff, though? It was peanuts.

He saw Lucy had listed the price to replace each piece of equipment, as well as what similar items had gone for in recent auctions. The total was over a million dollars.

"It looks like you've got some decisions to make," he finally said.

"Not helpful," she hissed, pulling the paper back. "What do we do? Rescue the first few items at whatever the cost? Wait until the end and hope we win something?"

"I'd recommend the former option," he said. "You've got money to spend. Set your limits, but try to get your wins in early. Get as much equipment as you can, then figure out the rest."

"Easy for you to say."

He shrugged. "I know. I'm sorry. It's not ideal, but that's the reality of the situation."

Lucy let out a sigh and finished her last bit of fish. Like all of the pieces before, she covered it with an obscene amount of tartar sauce. It looked like each bite had more sauce than fish. Even the fries were more of a shovel for ketchup than anything else.

He couldn't stop staring. It was mesmerizing, in a way, watching how she ate.

"I'll figure something out," she said, squirting out what had to be at least a quarter cup of ketchup onto her plate. "Now what did you want from me in exchange for all that great advice?"

Rob wiped his hands on his napkin and pushed the rest of his meal aside. The salad was good, but a bit too lively for his stomach right now. "I need help looking around."

"For what?"

"Like I said, another business to revive."

The cashier stopped by and dropped off a refill for Lucy. She smiled and thanked him.

It was the first time he'd seen her actually smile. He thought on this a moment too long before lifting his water glass to request a refill, but the cashier was gone.

"Do you have a list of targets?" she asked.

He shook his head. He wasn't going to fall for that. She would warn all the business to steer clear of him. "I don't have a list," he lied. "I thought maybe I would just drive around and look at things."

"That's your plan? To drive around?"

He leaned forward. "I'm not pretending to be a master-mind here. I'm desperate."

She thought on this for a moment before answering. "Fine. Where should we start?"

What he was most interested in was that hotel, but there was a chance something nearby would work and be less of a hassle. "How about the east side of the island? Something near the park would be a big selling point."

She shrugged. "All right. Let's go."

He offered to drive and she didn't protest. They drove around for an hour, with Rob carefully avoiding The Grand Madrona Hotel while poking around all of the properties nearby.

They kept running into the same problem: private roads and driveways that were not welcoming to trespassers.

"Driving up this road any further seems like a good way to get shot," he commented, staring down a large DO NOT ENTER sign.

Lucy laughed. "Nah, I know everyone around here. They won't shoot me. You, maybe, but not me."

"That's comforting."

"It doesn't matter," she continued. "I don't think there any old businesses around here."

"No? They can't all be private homes."

Lucy shrugged. "They are. People like their privacy."

"So there's nothing?"

"Just the hotel, but it doesn't need to be rescued." She paused. "Actually, there are a few old farms around here, but they're small. They've been out of commission for years. One was a beekeeper's property. He used to sell honey. There was a shop there, but he's mostly given it up."

That didn't sound promising, but it was something. "Can we go and look?"

"Sure."

Lucy directed him down a series of private roads until they reached a large, overgrown lot. "This looks terrible," he said as he got out of the car.

Lucy followed, slamming her door shut. "Yeah, I know. The farm next door isn't much better. The roof of the old barn collapsed and a few years ago, the main house burned down."

"They didn't rebuild?"

She shook her head. "No. I think they will eventually. We know the owners, and – "

"We?" he asked.

"My mom, Claire, and her boyfriend, Chip. He knows everyone. He's lived here for years."

"I thought you were the one who knew everyone."

She flashed a smile. "I've only been here a few months, but yeah, I make friends wherever I go."

He was pretty sure she was being sarcastic, but he wasn't going to challenge her on it. He watched as she walked out into the tall grass, almost disappearing.

Rob followed. She had her cell phone out, showing a map of the area.

"See this? That's how big the farm used to be. Right next door is the old beekeeper's property."

"How big is that?"

"Eh..." She zoomed in, then out again. "I don't know, five acres? Not enough for you."

He shook his head. "No. That's a small operation."

She pointed to some trees on the map due south of The Grand Madrona Hotel. "This area here is just an old house no one has lived in for over a decade. It used to be this grand estate, but it's abandoned now. I think the owner died and his kids fought over it, so it just fell apart."

"That's a shame," Rob said, but he was hardly listening.

The wheels in his head were turning. He'd been unable to find any flaw with the hotel itself, but it seemed that nearly every property around it was falling apart and in disrepair.

This was the solution he'd been looking for. Abandoned homes, shackled businesses, and near total deterioration.

Or, to put more simply, blight. Something he could work with. Something the hotel wouldn't be able to fight. If he played his cards right, they'd get an even bigger piece of land than they'd initially hoped for.

"Sorry to disappoint you," Lucy said, walking back toward the car.

Rob had to force himself to play it cool. He got to the car and opened the driver's door. "That's okay. It's getting dark. Maybe we can try again tomorrow?"

Chapter Fifteen

The trip was entirely worthless to Rob, just as Lucy had intended. She wasn't going to lead him to some struggling business so he could take it over or run it into bankruptcy. Why would she allow another islander to suffer the fate of Grindstone Farm?

There was an unintended consequence of their drive, however. Lucy had an idea. A *good* one.

The dilapidated farm and run-down honey shop had gotten her thinking. Grindstone wasn't the first business in history to come under attack. Owners fell on hard times, got sick, or simply couldn't keep up with the modern world. People – real people, not people like Rob – could share in that story. They sympathized. They empathized.

There had been enough sympathy to raise hundreds of thousands of dollars for Grindstone, and yet she hadn't thought to appeal to the farm's likely sympathetic neighbors about the auction.

Did they know how dire things were? Did they understand what the auction could do to the farm? Of course not, but only because it hadn't been explained to them.

Lucy could do that. She could explain. She was a fantastic communicator – that was one of the things on her resume that wasn't an exaggeration.

Rob wasn't terribly chatty as they drove back to her car. That was fine, because Lucy wasn't in the mood to make conversation. She assumed he was brooding, or envisioning his career imploding.

She almost felt bad for him, but there was no time to waste. They parted ways and she went straight home to find Lillian watching TV on the couch. Lucy descended upon her in a manically raving fashion, telling her about her idea.

"Slow down," Lillian said, ten minutes into the rant. "I think I'm missing some key information."

Lucy realized she'd been clutching her purse in her hand the entire time she was talking at Lillian. She released her grip and took a seat. "It's simple. Have you ever heard of penny auctions?"

"I don't think so," Lillian said with a shrug.

She took a deep breath. "Okay, back during the Great Depression, bankers were foreclosing on all of these farms and holding auctions."

"Sounds familiar."

Lucy nodded. "Right! It's not that different than what's happening to us. What was interesting, though, was that they'd try to hold auctions and all of the neighboring farmers would show up with pitchforks and rifles and things to scare the bankers off. They weren't violent, of course, but they'd sabotage the auctions. They'd start the bidding at a penny, and then bid two pennies, and then three, and on and on. At the end, they'd give everything back to the farmer who had lost everything."

"Ah," Lillian nodded slowly. "You're going to build a time machine and get some of those farmers' pennies."

"What?" Lucy stared at her. It took a moment to realize her sister was joking. "No, stop, listen. We need the islanders to do the same thing."

Lillian let out a laugh. "I know, I got what you were saying. You were just being so intense that I felt like I needed to break the – "

Lucy cut her off. "I'm intense because we're running out of time!"

"Do you and I count as islanders?" asked Lillian. "I guess I don't, because I just got here, but you – "

Lucy waved a hand. "We don't matter. We're just two people. We need a hundred people. Two hundred. I don't know."

"It's not the worst idea," Lillian said slowly. "How will you get that many people, though?"

Lucy paused. "I don't know. I think I should talk to the local papers, and maybe go to the county council meeting. We can hand out flyers explaining what's going on and about the penny auctions? Get an old-timey picture on top, make it a thing, you know?"

"I can help with that!" Lillian said brightly.

"Good. I was hoping you would."

Lucy couldn't stop smiling. Despite the teasing, it would be wonderful to get help from Lillian. She was trustworthy, and though she didn't agree with Lucy's worries about Claire's health, Lillian would be helpful there, too.

It seemed like Claire had been doing okay, but Lucy couldn't let herself get caught up in farm excitement again and miss something important. Claire wasn't forthcoming about her health – Lucy had to ask specific questions to get information.

It was almost as though Claire thought it was best to deal with all health scares on her own and only update them later. It was a strange system, and Lucy dreaded hearing something like, "Oh, I was in the hospital for four days, but I didn't want to worry you."

The old "I didn't want to worry you" was a classic martyr mother tactic, and Claire was an Olympic gold medalist in martyring.

Getting Lillian involved would be good. It might even free up some of Lucy's time so she could also keep an eye on Rob. She didn't know what he was up to, but she didn't like it – and she wouldn't let him get away with sneaking around, either.

Lucy continued meeting with Rob over the next two weeks, sporadically hopping into his car and expertly steering him away from any businesses that might be vulnerable to his schemes.

He never caught on to what she was doing. He was a dunce, and kept wasting his time in trying to get to know her.

Lucy avoided answering most of his personal questions. She had no intention of letting him in or giving him a hint to how she worked.

Rob, on the other hand, didn't seem to have any hang-ups. He was more than willing to talk about himself and his past, and since he was seemingly the loneliest man on Orcas Island, he kept offering to help her prepare for the auction.

Lucy declined all of his help until the day before the event, when Rob showed up at Grindstone and asked if she was up for a drive.

"I can't," she said. "I have a lot of last-minute things to do."

Though she'd had two weeks, time had gotten away from her, as it always did. She'd planned too much and was starting to feel the pressure.

"Let me help," he said. "I know almost as much about the auction as you do."

She eyed him warily. Was that a hint he'd been doing his own research?

"You talk about it so much," he added.

Well, she'd had to talk about *something*. "Oh. Yeah. Sorry for boring you."

"It's – I wasn't bored, I've enjoyed it. What can I do to help?"

She shook her head. "You wouldn't be good at it."

A smile cracked on his face. "Is that so?"

"Yes," she said, digging through a stack of boxes until she found the one she was looking for.

She dragged it onto the farm shop counter and let out a breath. When she looked up, she saw him staring at her, arms crossed.

The sight of him made Lucy burst out into a laugh. She hadn't meant to poke at his competitive streak. He looked quite determined.

"Why don't you try me?" he finally said.

She let out a sigh, opening the lid to the box. "Fine. I printed out these pamphlets to explain the auction situation to people on the islands. I meant to get them mailed out, but I missed the deadline, and then I figured it would be better to hand them out in person, but now I'm a little short on time."

He smirked. "You think?"

"See? This is why I don't ask you to help. I don't need your attitude."

He rushed to correct himself. "Oh, come on. Please? I can do this. You think I haven't gone door to door before?"

"Doing what? Selling timeshares?"

"Worse. Selling knives no one wanted."

Lucy cringed. "Sounds like a pyramid scheme."

"It was." He grabbed a pamphlet from the pile. "I bet I could hit more houses than you can."

Lucy snatched the pamphlet out of his hand. "Yeah, right."

"I could. I'll bet you twenty bucks."

The extra set of hands would be helpful, and it wasn't like he could sabotage her pamphlets...

She cleared her throat. "Fifty bucks."

"Deal."

They shook on it and she heaved a box into his arms. "You can help me carry these."

"Where should I start?"

She walked out to her car and he followed. "Marty and Emma are doing Orcas Island, and my friend Margie is doing San Juan with her husband and daughters."

"What does that leave?"

She let out a disgusted sigh. "How do you *still* not know the other islands?"

He shrugged. "I've been busy."

"We'll go to Lopez, and I think that'll be all we can do for the day."

"Sounds great." He loaded the box into Lucy's trunk and slammed it shut. "Should we get a flight there to save time?"

Lucy stopped and spun to look at him. "Absolutely not. I'm not flying anywhere."

He smiled at her, amused. "Why not?"

She got into the driver's seat and started the car.

Rob followed her lead, a goofy smile still on his face. "We could drop the pamphlets from the air."

"No. That's littering."

He nodded. "Fair point. Alternatively, we could fly a banner on the back of the – "

"No!" She turned to him. "Are you done?"

Rob forced himself to look serious. "Yes. I'm ready to win this bet."

Unbelievable.

She turned on some music and started the drive to the ferry.

Chapter Sixteen

The day of the auction finally arrived, and Lillian was awakened at four that morning by the clanking of pots and pans.

She wandered into the kitchen to find Lucy crafting a multi-course breakfast for them while also trying to rally a last bit of support from the local Facebook groups and making phone calls to people who were clearly still asleep.

Lillian had expected a rampage like this. She was ready for it.

Well, most of it. The Facebook fight Lucy had gotten into at six that morning was an unexpected bump in the road. Lillian had managed to get Lucy away from the computer after only fifteen minutes of arguing, which wasn't bad.

It was her own mistake for not intercepting it earlier. Lillian had foolishly thought she could get up at seven and still have the Lucy situation under control.

Her plan had to be adapted once she walked into the kitchen and saw the pile of waffles, a bowl of hard-boiled eggs, and a plate of sausage and biscuits. Lucy had her battle station set up at the kitchen table, with stacks of papers balanced precariously between rows of coffee mugs.

They ate breakfast quickly, then Lillian got busy packing the leftovers away. They'd have enough breakfasts for the rest of the week, maybe two. Lillian was debating making breakfast sandwiches from the biscuits and freezing them when she heard Lucy let out a giggle.

"Is everything okay?" she asked.

Lucy didn't look up from her computer screen. "Yes. I mean, no. It looks like the ferries from Anacortes were all canceled this morning."

Lillian poured herself a cup of coffee and took a seat. The breakfast sandwich situation could be figured out later. "And why did that make you giggle like a crazy person?"

"Because any non-islanders who wanted to come to the auction are going to have a harder time getting here."

Lillian took a sip of coffee as she processed this information. "Hang on. Am I to understand that *you* are responsible for the ferry cancellations?"

"I can't be held responsible for that," Lucy said with a smile. "Ferry travel is fickle. These people would know that if they had ever set foot on the island before. The weather can be bad, employees can get sick. Who knows what really happened?"

"*Lucy!* People depend on those ferries. You can't just – "

Lucy cut her off. "I know, I know. I didn't ask them to do it! Maybe I *hinted*, but I didn't ask."

Lillian stared at her. "Unbelievable."

Lucy turned back to her screen, suppressing a smile. "There have been reports of irate stranded passengers demanding to be taken to Orcas Island."

She knew she shouldn't encourage Lucy, but she couldn't help it. She laughed.

"How about we go on a nice, relaxing walk?" Lillian suggested. "We can go anywhere you want. To the bakery, maybe? Are you still hungry?"

Lucy shook her head. "I'm fine, but thanks."

"You know, they say the best time to relax is when you don't have the time to relax."

"Uh huh."

"Relaxation is important," Lillian continued. She should've rehearsed this. It didn't seem to be working. "You don't want to be so worked up that you faint in the middle of the auction or something."

Lucy stopped what she was doing and turned to face her. "That would actually be a good distraction. Maybe keep people from bidding."

Oh dear. Lucy was too far gone. Lillian would have to go along with whatever she had planned and be supportive. She was good at that.

She'd taken the day off from work, so it wouldn't be too hard to follow Lucy's whims. Her job was flexible, which was lovely in situations like these. Normally, Lillian didn't need much flexibility – her boyfriend Mason traveled so much that her schedule was quite mundane.

Before, she'd worked as a social worker at a hospital. Her schedule had been much more hectic then. Now, she got to work from home and do the same sort of job, calling patients after they'd already left the hospital.

She did everything from finding specialists for follow up, to navigating bills, to even helping the patients get rides to their appointments.

It was rewarding work and people appreciated her help. Best of all, Lillian had built a plethora of skills in helping people during a time of crisis. Lucy's situation wasn't quite the same as someone who had just had a long and difficult hospitalization, but her feelings were quite similar.

"I've gotta run," Lucy said, snapping her laptop shut and almost tripping as she hopped toward the door. "I need to set things up at the farm."

"Hang on," Lillian said. "Are you going to be the one bidding today?"

Lucy shook her head. "I'm leaving that power in Fiona's hands. I don't deserve it, and to tell you the truth, I don't know if I can handle it."

"That's wise." Lillian wasn't too worried about letting Lucy leave. She seemed to at least be acknowledging her limits. "I'll be at the farm soon to help. I'm glad we won't be seeing that power go to your head."

Lucy made a face before grabbing her bag and walking out the door.

It didn't take long for Lillian to get ready, and Marty swung by to pick her up. They got to the farm quickly, despite Marty's concern that Lucy may have had the roads shut down.

To the contrary, the parking lot was quite full.

"This is interesting," Lillian said as she got out of the car.

Marty stood gaping for a moment. "I've never seen this many people gathered in one place on this island."

"That's a bad sign, isn't it?"

He frowned. "I don't know."

The auction didn't start for another two hours and Lillian wanted to find a way to be useful, but it proved more difficult than she'd expected.

Eventually they found Lucy and managed to stop her for a moment.

"Please," Lillian said, "what can we do to help?"

"I don't know." Lucy stood, a hand on her forehead and her hair blowing wildly in the wind. "I'm nervous about all of the people here."

"I'm sure it'll be okay," Lillian said unconvincingly.

Lucy dropped her voice. "Could you go and talk to some of them? See if they're here to bid, or just here for moral support?"

"I'm here for moral support," Marty offered.

Lucy ignored him and continued. "Ask them which items they're interested in. No, wait! Ask if they have any questions. Yeah, do that! Then you can figure out if they're being honest."

"I don't know that this is a good task for me," Marty said. "I'm not good at socializing, even when it's not early in the morning."

Lucy shot a pleading glance at Lillian. "Please?"

Lillian didn't like the idea either, but she wasn't going to say no. "Of course."

At that moment, Lillian's phone went off.

"Sorry, one second." She pulled it out of her pocket and stepped away.

It was Mason!

"Hey!"

"Hey, where are you?" he asked. "I just got home a few days early and thought we could get breakfast. Or lunch, if you're busy."

"Ah, I'm not near home."

"What? Why?"

"I'm on Orcas Island, remember?"

Mason let out a groan. "Oh, that's right. Your mom and the stroke and the whole thing. How's she doing?"

"She's good. That's all fine. Remember I told you I stayed to help Lucy with her farm auction?"

"Oh, right, right." There was some noise from his end. It sounded like he was getting into the car. "I'm sorry. Farms are just boring to me, so I forgot about it."

Typical. "I know."

"I guess I'll hang out with one of the guys instead. When are you coming back?"

She looked up to see Lucy bickering with Marty, pointing a finger into his chest and then wagging it in his face.

Hilarious. The two of them were like brother and sister. Lillian couldn't decide who was the older sibling. They seemed to alternate who was more ridiculous. "I'm not sure when I'll be ready to leave. I think they still need me."

"Well, let me know. Good luck with the farm stuff!"

She thanked him and ended the call. It was disappointing he'd forgotten what she had told him, but to be fair, he'd been busy with work and farms weren't at the top of his priority list.

She rejoined Lucy and Marty. "Do I need to break this up? What's the problem?"

"Nothing." Lucy waved a hand. "Just a disagreement between friends. Who was that?"

"Mason."

"Aw! Was he calling to wish us good luck?"

"Yeah." Lillian cleared her throat. "He was just letting me know he's back. He was on a work trip for the last two weeks."

"What does he do?" Marty asked.

"He's a chemical engineer for an oil company."

"Where does he travel?"

Lillian let out a sigh. "Everywhere, it seems. He has to go on site a lot and is gone for weeks at a time."

"Good," Lucy concluded. "So he didn't miss you too much."

That was one way to look at it. "Luckily not."

"While you were gone, Lucy decided what we needed to say to people," Marty said.

"Is that right?" Lillian smiled at her. "What will I be saying?"

"Marty will fill you in," she said, walking off. "Get talking!"

She watched as Lucy disappeared, and Marty turned to face her.

He had a face of mock solemnity. "I tried to save you, but the best I could do was tell her that having you pretend to be a reporter was a bad idea."

Lillian laughed. "I'll stick with asking if they have any questions. What are you going to say?"

"Hopefully nothing." Marty shrugged. "Lucy says I have a knack for always saying the wrong thing."

"That's not true!"

Marty seemed unbothered by it. He was still smiling. "I'll be your moral support. No – I'll be the muscle!"

The muscle. Right. Very useful.

Lillian decided not to tease him about it. While she wasn't as shy as he was, it was still mortifying to walk up to strangers and start conversations.

In order to psych herself up, Lillian told herself she was a representative of Grindstone Farm, because technically she was.

Her first attempt was with an older guy who was eyeing one of the tractors. "Hi there, I'm Lillian, and this is Marty. I wanted to see if you had any questions about the items up for auction today?"

The man smiled at her. "No, thank you, miss. I'm here to show my support. I've got a farm on Lopez and I hate to see what's happening to Grindstone."

"Thank you for coming out," Marty said before walking away.

Lillian smiled and thanked the man before running after Marty. It had been a bit awkward, but not as bad as she'd expected. She used the same line on the next person, then the next.

A few declined her help, but many of them echoed the first man, saying they weren't there to bid on anything. It was quite remarkable.

After half an hour of chatting, Lillian was excited to report back to Lucy. They found her in the farm shop arguing with a tall guy.

Lillian recognized him from a website Lucy had showed her one night when she claimed he was "out to get them."

Rob. He was even more handsome in person, all neat and tidy in a rich, blue button-down shirt and grey slacks. Did he always dress that nicely?

"The bet was fifty dollars, period," Lucy said, digging in her purse. "Not fifty dollars *and* bragging rights."

"I didn't come here to claim my prize," Rob said innocently. "I'm here to support Grindstone."

"Sure you are," she snapped. "I'd prefer it if you supported us from the safety of your fish office."

Fish office? What on earth was she going on about now?

Rob accepted a handful of cash from Lucy. "I needed a break."

"Are you selling off the farm already?" Marty asked. "I'd still like to buy that slingshot."

Lucy glared at him. "I'm settling a bet."

Rob introduced himself, but before Lillian or Marty could reply, Lucy spoke again. "Yes, fine, there's no time for that. What did you guys find out?"

Lillian had been listening to Lucy complain about Rob for weeks. She wondered when she'd finally meet him, and now that he was here, there was no need to be rude. "I'm Lucy's sister, Lillian, and this is our cousin, Marty."

"Nice to meet you," Rob said.

Lucy shot him an annoyed look as Lillian went on. "Mostly good news, I think. We talked to a lot of people who said they're here to be supportive."

Lucy's eyes lit up. "Really?"

Marty nodded. "Yeah. There's even a farmer here from Lopez. Whatever you guys did worked."

"See?" Rob turned to Lucy. "I told you it was worth the time to look for actual farmers."

"That wasn't your idea," Lucy said.

Rob turned to Marty and lowered his voice. "She's angry because I still hit more houses than she did."

Lucy let out a disgusted sigh. "For all you know, that could've been a farmer whom I talked to. People like me better. That's why it took me longer to get through the same number of houses, because people actually wanted to talk to me."

"That may be true," Rob said with a nod, "but being better-liked wasn't part of the bet."

Lillian stifled a laugh. No wonder Lucy couldn't stand this guy. He was playing her like a fiddle.

Marty, apparently oblivious to the fight in front of them, interjected. "I think you've got a decent shot at getting what you need to get. We didn't meet anyone who seemed super keen on robbing the place blind."

"It only takes one banker to weasel their way in and ruin our plans," Lucy said as she paced the room.

Rob cocked his head to the side. "Was that directed at me?"

Lillian bit her lip. This was hilarious. Rob was winding Lucy up, and better yet, he seemed to be good at it. How was Marty missing this?

She looked over at him. He had picked up a book from the shelf and was leafing through it.

"I don't know. You're the one who showed up looking like a banker," Lucy hissed. "Don't you own any other clothes?"

Rob's face fell slack and his eyes wandered up innocently. "No. None at all. This is my only pair of pants."

Lucy's phone went off and she let out a shriek. "All right, kids, it's almost go time. Let's move!"

Chapter Seventeen

They followed Lucy into the open field where the auction was to take place. Rob wasn't one to get nervous easily, but Lucy's explosive anxiety was starting to breach his walls.

It didn't look good. There was a huge turnout, well over a hundred people, and despite what Lillian had said, not all of them were friends.

They were joined by an older man and woman whom Lillian introduced as Claire and Chip.

"It's nice to meet you." Rob offered a handshake to Claire first. "I've heard so much about you."

That wasn't true, of course. Lucy never told him anything. It had become a game for him to try to get any information about her life. Perhaps this group would be more illuminating.

"We've heard about you, too," Chip said, returning the handshake.

Rob caught what he thought was a look from Chip and decided to see if he could figure out what it meant. "Would you say what you've heard about me have been complaints?"

Chip stared straight ahead at the auctioneer. "If you have to ask, you already know."

They both laughed, unnoticed by the rest of the group. Claire and Lillian were huddled together, whispering, and Marty was texting.

Rob was looking around at the crowd when he caught Marty's eye.

He put his phone into his pocket and walked over. "So, Rob, how did you get involved with the farm?"

Best to keep it general. "My company was trying to buy the farm's debt to restructure it. Do you work in finance?"

"I don't," Marty said. "And I can't say I know much about restructuring debt."

Good. Rob preferred if no one knew what he was there for. True, he wasn't after Grindstone anymore, but surely Lucy, who believed in the power of community, wouldn't appreciate what he was about to do to that hotel.

Even if she found out and wanted to stop him, it was too late. When Rob told his boss about the plan to declare the area blighted, he immediately got a team of five people to help with the paperwork.

It was complicated and tricky, but they had swiftly gathered all the evidence needed to prove the area needed to be condemned. Under eminent domain law, their proposed development plan to improve the properties would seal the deal.

If all went well, they would send certified letters to the property owners next week informing them of the final action: a vote by the county to condemn the area.

If Lucy caught wind of it, she wouldn't like it. Hopefully she wouldn't try to take it up as her next cause. It would be a disappointment for her. Rob and his team had done everything by the book, and eminent domain was nearly impossible to fight. Also, he was really enjoying spending time with her, and he didn't want to start a fight.

Lucy rejoined their group just as an announcement rang out that the auction was about to begin. She jumped at this and ran off again, finding Fiona in the crowd.

The first items up for auction were the farm's three copper pot stills. Rob didn't know much about farm equipment, but he knew these were for apple whiskey distillation. As a bonus, they looked kind of snazzy, all shining in the sun. He could see a partner at OSS buying one to display at a party. A waste of money, of course, but partners had plenty of money to waste.

The betting didn't start terribly low, unfortunately for Grindstone, but it didn't go far either. Fiona placed the first bid, and despite the auctioneer trying to press the price up, no one spoke. Fiona won the first pot still, and the little group surrounding Rob cheered quietly.

They repeated the process for the other two pot stills and then moved on to the other whiskey-making equipment. These weren't as cool looking and Rob didn't know what the pieces were called, but he paid attention as a small bidding war broke out for a fermentor and a bottler.

Fiona fought fiercely, but ultimately gave in on the bottler. It was her first loss, but from what Rob could see, she didn't seem overly torn up about it.

The auction went on for another thirty minutes, with Grindstone winning almost every item at a bargain cost. It was going well until the apple harvester came up for auction.

Lucy had mentioned this one might be tough to keep. A new apple harvester retailed for a hundred and thirty thousand dollars; however, Grindstone had gotten this one at just over half that price.

The bidding started with Fiona, but quickly escalated to a hundred thousand dollars, bouncing between four other attendees.

Once it hit one hundred and twenty-five thousand, Fiona stepped back. Rob stared at her, trying to read her expression. She was calm and collected, studying the sheet in front of her.

The auctioneer called out that the price was going once.

Fiona looked up.

"Going twice!"

She frowned, murmured something to the man standing next to her, and nodded.

"Sold!"

Rob tried to catch sight of Lucy's face, but it was impossible. She was huddled with Fiona and the group, her back to him, whispering.

His heart sank. Hopefully Lucy wasn't too upset. Maybe she had a plan for getting another one?

The auction went on, and Lucy rejoined them for the last item: a large tractor.

"Well?" asked Claire. "How are you feeling? How's Fiona?"

"Good. And no one cares about that old tractor," she said confidently. "We did pretty well. Not great, since we lost the harvester, but one of the guys is pretty sure we can afford another one."

"Will the farm live on?" Lillian asked.

Lucy beamed. "I think it will."

"I'm so proud of you!" Claire said, pulling Lucy in for a hug.

"Thank you." She broke out of the hug and looked at Rob. "I bet Carriageway is furious that the bidding didn't go higher on everything."

Marty cocked his head to the side. "Why?"

"Because I thought they get all of the profits as part of the bankruptcy deal?"

Rob watched as everyone's eyes slowly drifted to him. He cleared his throat. "Maybe, maybe not. To be honest, I don't see a representative here from Carriageway, so they're probably past the point of caring."

Lucy's face hardened, the smile disappearing as though it had never existed. "Do you have to ruin everything?"

He paused. "I thought that would be a good thing?"

Her only response was to glare at him, and Lillian stepped in to fill the silence. "At least Rob didn't try to outbid you for all that stuff."

Lucy crossed her arms. "I guess."

He turned to Lucy, studying her pinched face. How could she be so sour after such a success? Had she really thought he was here to bid?

"Lucy," he said slowly. "Were you afraid I was going after the farm equipment?"

"Afraid isn't the right word." Lucy rolled her eyes and laughed. "More like I didn't trust you."

He smiled. "Ah. That's much better then."

Claire, a smile dancing on her lips, cleared her throat. "Dinner tonight? I have a table saved at the restaurant."

"Yes!" Lucy clapped her hands, recovering from her salty mood. "I'll go and tell Fiona and the gang."

"What time?" Marty asked.

"Eight," Lucy said. "At the hotel. Will Emma be able to come?"

Marty nodded. "Yeah. We'll be there."

Lillian grabbed Lucy's arm, stopping her from leaving. "It'd be polite if you invited your friend, too."

She stopped to look at Rob.

Clearly, she didn't consider him a friend. Rob's heart sunk at the thought. He didn't even mind if Lucy kept blasting fire at him with her words – he just liked being in her company. She was funny, whip-smart, and had achieved a near miracle with this farm.

She was also beautiful, but that wasn't something he could allude to without having his head bitten off.

Not yet, at least.

"Do you want to celebrate our victory?" Lucy asked.

"That would be nice." He paused, adding, "I am happy for you, whether you believe it or not."

"Eight o'clock at The Plum Spoon," she said, turning and pulling Lillian away.

"Where is that?" he asked.

"Right in the lobby of Claire's hotel."

Oh right. He'd forgotten Claire was involved with a hotel on the island. She might not appreciate him going after one of the hotels, but on the other hand, she might be appreciative of him taking out one of her competitors.

"Is it called Claire's Hotel?" he called out.

"No. It's The Grand Madrona." Lucy called over her shoulder as she walked off. "Don't be late."

Chapter Eighteen

It was *finally* over.

All of a sudden, it felt like Lucy was moving in slow motion. Though her chest felt light, her limbs were heavy, and her skin was suddenly cold.

There was still work to be done, though. She broke off from Lillian and updated Fiona and the rest of the crew about dinner plans. After that, Lillian wanted to get lunch in town, but Lucy couldn't imagine sitting upright in a restaurant.

Instead, she drove straight back to her apartment, walked through the front door, and collapsed onto her bed.

She awoke three hours later. It took her a minute to remember what had happened, and when she did, she smiled and whispered, "Check and mate."

It hadn't been a perfect victory, but it was still a win in her book. They'd managed to save the most important equipment, and they had a plan for how to pay for the rest of what they needed. The most tense moment for Lucy had been when some stranger started bidding on the goats.

She'd taken that personally and planned to outbid them, no matter the personal cost. Luckily, Fiona managed to edge the guy out.

Lucy rose from bed slowly, rubbing her face and yawning. She'd fallen into bed fully clothed, and just now she was realizing her pants had sprays of mud on them.

Farms. Ugh.

She took them off and tossed them into her laundry basket before getting into the shower.

When she finally got herself to the kitchen, Lillian was waiting for her.

"You're alive!" Lillian stood from her seat at the kitchen table. She had her work laptop set up, but didn't seem particularly involved with it. "I had pizza for lunch. I saved you some, if you're hungry."

Food had not crossed her mind at all, but now she had a hard time ignoring the gnawing hole in her stomach. "Thanks, Lil!"

Lucy pulled the fridge door open and saw the slices basking under the dull light in all their glory – the cheese hardened, the mushrooms and onions dry and stiff, the crust dusted with flour.

Cold pizza. Heaven.

She pulled the plate out and took a seat at the table. "How did you know exactly what I needed?"

"I'm just good like that," Lillian said. "Are you feeling okay?"

Lucy had to swallow before she could respond. She was eating like a starved woman, taking bites that were far too big. "Yeah, I'm fine. I kinda crashed after the auction, but I'm good now. I was working off very little sleep."

"I know. It seemed like you were running purely on excitement and a touch of rage."

"My special blend," Lucy said, her mouth again full of pizza.

They laughed. "Do you know if everyone from Grindstone will come to dinner tonight?"

"I think so. The plan is to get all of the equipment back in the place tomorrow. It's too much to do in one day."

"That makes sense."

Lucy set the dry crust on her plate and stood. She needed water before she could tackle it. "Thanks for inviting Rob, by the way."

Lillian smiled. "You were being so rude to him! He doesn't seem that bad."

"Don't be fooled. He's conniving."

"He didn't bid on anything," Lillian said, in her even-toned-Lillian-voice. "What do you have against him now?"

Lucy was sure there were things, but she just didn't know what they were yet. How was she supposed to explain that to Lillian, who'd rarely met a person she didn't like or couldn't defend? "He gives off a bad vibe."

"A bad vibe?" Lillian paused. "You mean he pushes your buttons?"

"He does not push my buttons!" She didn't even know what that was supposed to mean. It just seemed like she should disagree with Lillian, and quickly. "He's an outsider."

Lillian shrugged. "So are we."

"It doesn't matter." Lucy waved a hand and filled up a glass of water.

"I'm betting he doesn't have any other friends on the island," Lillian continued. "It wouldn't kill you to at least try to be polite."

Lucy crossed her arms. "Why do you have to be so nice to everyone?"

She smiled, eyes back on her computer. "I'm just a sucker like that, I guess."

As much as Lucy wanted to ignore Lillian's comments, they nagged at her. That evening, when she saw Rob walk into The Grand Madrona, she told herself she should try to be nice.

"Were you waiting for me?" he asked when he spotted her.

How presumptive. "No. I think I just have bad timing."

"Yes, terrible," he said with a smile.

What was that supposed to mean? She could feel herself bristling, but Lillian's face floated into her mind's eye and stopped her from speaking.

Try to be *nice*.

Rob stood in front of The Plum Spoon, looking it up and down from ceiling to floor. "This place looks cool."

Why was he inspecting it like that? That wasn't how a normal person looked at a restaurant.

She quieted her thoughts and nodded. "It is cool. Thanks for coming."

"Thanks for letting me come. I haven't gotten much human interaction in the last few weeks."

"Doesn't me driving around with you count?"

He stopped looking around and turned to her. "Of course. That's been the highlight of my stay."

If he meant it, that was quite sad. Perhaps Lillian was right about him not having any friends. "After you."

They walked in and Lucy was surprised to find nearly everyone from the farm was already there. The restaurant usually had a quiet, sophisticated atmosphere. Now, however, it was filled with raucous laughter and the symphony of voices, each trying to talk over the next. The party had started early.

Lucy would've preferred to be in the middle of the action, but it was too late. Fiona and the rest of the farm staff had taken over much of the long table, and their loud conversations were impossible to penetrate. Lucy barely got in a hello as she sat down, stuck at the end of the table with Rob.

A waiter came by to drop off an oyster appetizer and get their drink orders. Lucy ordered a glass of red wine and tried to listen to the discussion at the middle of the table – something about the ferry workers – and Rob apparently followed her lead.

"Was that your doing? Getting the ferries canceled?" he asked.

She took an oyster onto her plate. "I can't take credit for the idea."

Rob reached forward and grabbed an oyster for himself. "But?"

Always prying, wasn't he? "But...I might have talked to some people, and things happened from there."

He smiled. "Impressive."

"Don't patronize me," Lucy said, dislodging her oyster with a fork before sucking it down.

Rob put his hands up. "I'm not! What you did with the farm was something I've never seen before. Most auctions don't turn out that way. In fact, I've never seen one where the old owners aren't completely cleaned out."

She shifted in her seat. His compliments seemed genuine, which made her more uncomfortable than when he was sarcastic. "That's too bad for those farmers."

"I agree. Something's been bothering me about it, though."

She felt her heart leap. Here it was. He was going to show his hand. She took a sip of water as naturally as she could. "Oh?"

"Yes. I have a serious question for you." He set his fork down. "You don't have to answer it if you don't want to."

As if she would feel pressured to tell him anything. Lucy grabbed another oyster. "Okay."

"Now that you've saved the farm, do you want to quit again?"

Dang it. Not the exposé she'd been hoping for. And yet...

She couldn't help but smile. She hadn't thought about it, but now that he'd brought it up, quitting seemed like the logical next step.

Lucy dropped her voice. "Kind of. Why? Do you have a job for me?"

"No, but I'm sure you could get any number of jobs after what you just pulled off."

Ha. As if she needed help *getting* jobs. "That's not the problem. I've worked in marketing, graphic design, and logistics. I had a brief stint at a quilting shop, and a few weeks at gym startup – that was the weirdest one, actually."

He sat back, staring at her. "Why do you jump around so much?"

"I'm easily bored, and I like a challenge," she said simply. "Are you a company man? One company until the day you die?"

He shook his head. "Only if I can maximize my success there."

"Maximize success?" Lucy snorted a laugh. "What does that even mean?"

"Making partner," he said, attempting to scoop the inside of his oyster with a spoon. It escaped him, the shell wildly shooting across the plate.

"Ah. Making partner." She took a sip of red wine. Claire wasn't cheaping out on them – this was the good stuff. "Is that what you believe will make you happy?"

He stopped his oyster hunt to look up at her. "In a way, yes. Does moving from job to job make you happy?"

"Yes," she said firmly. "It does."

Lucy stared at him, and he stared back.

After an uncomfortably long time, he broke eye contact. "You said your mom works at the hotel?"

"You could say that." Lucy grabbed a slice of apple topped with brie and popped it into her mouth. "She owns it."

Rob's oyster shell hit his plate with a loud clatter. "Sorry," he murmured, grabbing it quickly.

He then tried to poke the fleshy innards with a spoon, only for it to fall to his plate with a splat.

Lucy couldn't stop staring. It was like a car crash in slow motion – an oyster crash. His cheeks actually flushed pink as he tried to scoop the slimy bugger without using anything but a spoon.

How long had he been struggling with that one oyster? Lucy felt sorry for him for a moment. He looked like an overgrown child trying to get food into his mouth.

"You really just want to dislodge them and then sip them out," she said. "Once one gets away, it can be hard to chase it."

"I'm seeing that," he said with a laugh. He finally stabbed the oyster with a fork and got it safely into his mouth. "I'm not big on seafood."

She nodded. "That does make island living tough."

"Ha, yeah." He flashed a smile. "Has your mom always been in the hotel business?"

Lucy took another sip of wine only to notice her glass was empty. That had gone down quickly. "No. This is all new for her. She used to be a paralegal."

"So she shares your love of job hopping?"

Lucy snickered. The thought of sensible Claire erratically moving from job to job was unimaginable. "No, Claire is far too levelheaded for that."

"That's still quite a jump."

"It is." Lucy paused. She didn't mean to make them both seem incapable of holding down a job. Claire could keep a job, at least. The jury was still out for Lucy. "It's a crazy story of how she got here."

Another oyster escaped him.

How had this rich kid eaten so few oysters in his life? Did he make his history up? Had his strict dad made him live on oatmeal and eggs until he was eighteen or something?

That would make a lot of sense, actually.

Rob cleared his throat. "Did you fundraise for her, too?"

"No." Lucy took a deep breath and forced a solemn look onto her face. "It all started when I was four."

"When you were four?" He set his spoon down, apparently abandoning his efforts to eat any more oysters.

She nodded. "My parents died in a plane crash that year."

His eyes widened, and his mouth briefly popped open. "Wow, I'm sorry."

Lucy flashed a look at Lillian, safely at the other end of the table. That wasn't nice of her to drop onto him, and she knew it.

"It's fine. It was a long time ago. My mom, Claire's sister Holly, died in the crash." Lucy paused. This story had only gotten more complicated in the last year. "We thought Claire's twin sister Becca died in the crash, too, but she didn't."

He opened his mouth, but stopped himself.

"What?" she asked.

"I can't tell if you're pulling my leg."

Lucy laughed. That was the price of her sarcasm. "I'm not."

She took a swig of water and told him the rest of the story – her uncle's inheritance going to Claire, buying the hotel, Marty showing up with the FBI on his tail, and Aunt Becca being discovered. All of it.

When she was done, she sat back and studied him.

Or at least, she tried to. His expression was unreadable. He could have been doing a crossword puzzle or listening to *Elmo's Song* on loop.

"So," she finally said, "you'll forgive me if I don't follow your idea of a good career track. Life is too short to stay at bad jobs."

"I agree. I like my job."

Of course he did. "That's good."

He hesitated before speaking again. "Also, I didn't – you don't have to explain yourself to me. That story is...I mean it's incredible."

She straightened in her seat. It was nice having an actual conversation with him. It didn't seem like he was out to get her, or trying to trick her. It didn't seem like he was capable of tricking her. He couldn't even get an oyster into his mouth.

"I don't know where I'm going next," she said. "I'd like to find something as fulfilling as this hotel has been for Claire, but so far, I've come up empty. At least I'm doing good deeds on my travels."

"Claire likes it here, then?"

"Oh yeah." Lucy sat back, taking a sip of wine. "It's given her a new purpose in life."

Rob started coughing, his face turning pink again.

"Are you okay?"

He nodded, still in a coughing fit. He managed to whisper, "Swallowed wrong."

"Ah." She looked around. He seemed to be dying in front of her eyes, but no one else was paying any attention. She pushed a glass of water toward him. "Here. Take a drink."

He nodded, doing as she'd instructed. The coughing slowed, though he was still struggling, doubled over in his seat.

She waited. After an eternity, he flashed a smile and said, "Excuse me," before rushing away from the table.

Chapter Nineteen

His dad always told him he didn't have the "killer instinct." Rob had spent the last ten years of his life trying to prove him wrong.

He'd found profit where no one else could. He worked hundred hour weeks, crushing his colleagues and taking promotion after promotion. He didn't negotiate or apologize – he got results.

Yet here, sharing dinner with a verifiable orphan at the very hotel he was about to destroy, he started to feel his nerve failing him.

Rob stumbled through the restaurant, spilling on to a patio that opened up to the sea.

There weren't many people outside, and the stars hung bright and clear above him.

He took a deep breath and closed his eyes.

It wasn't his fault the island was of interest to OSS and developers. If Rob didn't get them what they wanted, someone else would.

It wasn't his fault. It wasn't his problem.

And yet...

Claire's story felt like a bucket of water over his head. She wasn't some lowly employee at the hotel, like he'd tried to convince himself earlier. She wasn't a hot-shot hotel mogul. She was nothing short of a saint, adopting a trio of girls and working a low-paying job for years.

Lucy said this hotel had given her a purpose in life.

Purpose! Rob had never played a role in taking someone's purpose away.

Property, sure. Money, of course. But not purpose.

The coughing had stopped, but his throat was still on fire and nausea had settled into his stomach. He told himself it was the oyster, its slimy, cold blob of a body snailing its way down. He wanted to believe that, but all he could hear was his dad's voice.

"You're weak. I saw it when you were a kid, and I see it now. You don't have to be weak, but you choose to be again and again."

Rob could feel the weakness growing now as he argued with himself, debating if Claire would really miss the hotel, telling himself she'd get a fair price and be able to build something else.

It wasn't working.

He paced the patio as sweat dripped down his back. He couldn't go back in there and talk to Lucy. It was the first time she'd been civil to him, and it made him wonder if she somehow knew what he was doing.

Maybe she was plotting to have him killed? Arrested? Shipped off the island?

That was impossible. The letters couldn't have gone out yet. Maybe it wasn't too late to stop it. Rob pulled out his phone and called his boss.

Despite the late hour, he answered. "What's the news, Rob?"

That was how Rick answered the phone when he was in a bad – but not livid – mood. Rob spoke quickly. "I was hoping you could tell me. Did the letters go out yet?"

"No." A sigh. "We've run into some issues with zoning. We might have a problem."

"What kind of problem?" Rob's pulse quickened. It could fall apart, just like that, through no fault of his own. It was an out.

"I thought that was why you're calling. You haven't heard anything?"

"No, not yet." Rob cleared his throat. "What should I be doing?"

"Nothing for now. This is out of your depth. Hang tight and I'll let you know what EDT figures out."

EDT – the eminent domain team. That wasn't a good sign. They normally saved them for high-profile cases. "Got it."

"I'm busy. Anything else?"

"Nope. Thanks."

The call ended and Rob stared out over the water. It wasn't as hot outside as he'd thought. He wasn't sweating anymore.

The guilt, however, did not fade. The truth was, he hadn't known this was Claire's hotel. If he'd had known, he would've walked away. Now what was he going to do?

There was a chance Rick had brought in the EDT because things were so hopeless. Rob had come up with a good plan, but alas, if zoning was impossible, it was going to fall apart.

That would be the best of all possible outcomes. The deal would fizzle out and Lucy would never know what he'd done. Maybe his dad would call it weakness, but Rob was desperate for the deal to fall through and for Lucy to never find out about it.

"Rob?"

He spun around to see Lucy standing behind him. He forced a smile. "Hey."

"I wanted to make sure you weren't suffocating to death."

That was nice of her. Maybe she wasn't planning to have him killed. Not yet, at least. "I'm fine."

"Do you think it was the oyster?"

He laughed. "Yeah, I'm pretty sure it was. Thanks for checking on me."

"Your meal just arrived," she said. "Should we go back inside?"

He took a deep breath. It would all work out in the end. Lucy wouldn't go back to despising him. She might even grow to like him a little. He might even get to see that pretty smile again...

He cleared his throat. "Sure. Let's head back."

Chapter Twenty

It turned out to be a good thing Rob hadn't choked to death on an oyster the night of the farm auction. He seemed to loosen up after that, even going so far as to dress himself in regular clothes – jeans, chinos, and T-shirts.

He didn't go as far as wearing shorts, but Lucy appreciated the change. It was nice not having to hang out with a guy who looked like he was dressed to deny her a car loan. Plus, as not bad-looking as he was in a suit, he was just as not bad-looking in a fitted t-shirt.

He was still closer to "walked out of a catalog" than "average guy," but it worked. Lucy wondered if he'd bought the clothes on the island, or if he'd had them sent from his penthouse in New York City.

Even the material of his plain shirts looked nicer than anything she could buy on the island. She was tempted to reach out and feel one of the sleeves, just once, to see if his soft-looking shirt was cotton or some proprietary blend infused with silk.

She resisted, however, telling herself it was yet another symptom of her renewed boredom. She was so bored with her farm job that she'd started looking forward to seeing Rob.

They no longer took their island drives, instead spending their workdays together at the farm shop. Rob brought his laptop along, saying the fishy odor from the restaurant had grown unbearable and the music from the fitness classes were echoing in his dreams and driving him to madness.

Lucy didn't mind having him in the shop. They didn't have many customers this time of year, and since he was no longer a threat to the farm, Rob had become an amusing sounding board for her next set of schemes.

"What about cruise ships?" she asked him one day.

"What about them?" He sat back and crossed his arms. "I think they're an oversaturated industry."

As though she were thinking of investing in a cruise line. Lucy snorted. "What? I mean what do you think about me working on one? That'd be kind of cool, right? Like a vacation you don't have to pay for."

"Except you're not on vacation. You're working, and you're stuck on a ship with a bunch of needy people." He shook his head. "Actually, that sounds like a nightmare. You can never leave work."

"It can't be that bad. You get to go onto land sometimes, right? All the time, actually."

"Not the employees."

Lucy turned to rearrange the honey shelf for the third time that week. "I'd go onto land. Have you ever been on a cruise?"

"Not exactly."

His tone was off, and she turned to look at him. Rob was staring at his screen a bit too intently, like he was hiding something.

Lucy swooped in, hands on her hips. "What's that supposed to mean? Have you been on a cruise ship or not?"

"I've been on a ship." He hesitated. "Not a cruise ship."

Lucy let out a groan. That's why he was being weird. "It was a yacht, wasn't it? Your dad owns a yacht?"

"He does, but – "

"I knew it!" She pointed at him, cutting him off. "Of course you would think cruise ships aren't fun. You had your own private yacht growing up."

"I'd rather be on a ship with a thousand strangers than trapped on a ship with my dad," Rob said.

"How can he be that bad?" She took her seat behind the counter and logged into her laptop. "I'd put up with your dad if I could go on a yacht." She froze. "Wait, that's actually a good idea."

Rob eyed her wearily. "You want to work for my dad?"

"Why not?" She shrugged. "Maybe not him exactly, but someone like him. I could work on a yacht. At least there wouldn't be as many demanding customers."

"Believe me. One of my dad is worse than a thousand demanding customers."

"I don't buy it."

Rob sat back. "He was once so displeased with the chef he'd hired for a trans-Atlantic trip that he abandoned the guy in Cartagena."

Cartagena, Cartagena... Lucy had no idea where or what that was, but she didn't want to look uneducated. She'd search it online later. "What do you mean 'abandoned' him? Did he throw him overboard? I can swim."

Rob laughed. "No, he left him in port to teach him a lesson. The guy didn't have his passport or any of his stuff, which made it hard to get back to the US."

Lucy made a face. "Ew. Okay, that's pretty rude."

"It's more than rude. It's dangerous. My dad doesn't take kindly to human fault, and for some reason when he's on the boat, he becomes even more difficult."

Lucy frowned. Her history in customer service wasn't stellar. What kind of havoc could she wreak before being abandoned? "What if I keep my passport sewed into my clothes? Then I can live without fear."

"That would be something," Rob said, a half-smile on his lips.

"Or what if I managed to not get fired until we were in the middle of the ocean. What would he do to me then?"

He nodded. "That's happened, too. He had a helicopter come out and pick the person up."

"That doesn't sound so bad. Free helicopter ride."

"Not free." Rob stood and walked over to the counter, leaning toward her. "He'd send you the bill."

"Yikes. Was he one of those dads who made you pay rent when you turned twelve?"

Rob let out a laugh. "No. He wasn't like that. He was determined to give us the best of everything."

"But everyone else got treated like crap?"

He stared at the counter for a moment before looking up at her. "No, not everyone. He treated some staff generously. He paid for our nanny's kids to go to college."

"Wow."

Rob nodded. "Yeah. He's not a bad person. He's just... strongly principled."

"I don't know that purposefully abandoning someone without their passport is principled."

Rob nodded. "Fair. He's strict, then. Especially with himself. I can only imagine that he gave us all the stuff he would've wanted growing up."

"What was it you wanted growing up?"

"I just wanted to make him happy," Rob said with a shrug.

"I see."

Her view of Rob had evolved. He wasn't the villain she'd thought he was. He was just an overgrown kid still trying to impress his dad.

Parental relationships were so strange. Lucy often wondered how different she would be if her parents had been alive to raise her instead of Claire.

What mistakes would they have made? What blind spots would they have had? She had a hard time imagining either of them as anything but perfect.

"What about you?" he asked. "What complaints do you have about Claire?"

Lucy made a face. "Complaints?"

"Her flaws," Rob said.

"Claire doesn't really have flaws."

"Oh come on." Rob straightened, towering over her. "That can't be true."

The shirt he had on today was a lighter blue, not quite like a robin's egg, but in that color family. It made his eyes pop, and it looked so soft. His bicep was just in reach...

Lucy cleared her throat. "She's a bit of a martyr, I guess. I don't know if that's a flaw as much as it is a core trait."

"You're making me feel guilty that I made my dad sound so bad."

Lucy smiled. Maybe his dad just *was* bad. Claire would never do anything so cruel to a person, let alone someone who worked for her. Some of the hotel staff walked all over her. "I mean, she's not perfect. She's human. We fought a lot when I was a teenager, but who doesn't fight with their parents at that point?"

Rob looked down again, lost in thought. "I didn't really fight with my parents."

What a nerd. "What about your mom? You never talk about her."

"My mom?" He smiled. "She's a saint. She holds the family together when my dad is driving everyone crazy."

"Another martyr." Lucy let out a sigh. "Claire's always been a martyr. It was the hotel that finally changed her. Not a ton, but it's the only thing she's ever done for herself, and she's happy."

"That's good." Rob returned to his seat and reopened his laptop. "So you agree that's a no for the cruise ship?"

"Fine," Lucy said flatly. "I don't have any other ideas right now, though."

"You're going about it the wrong way," he said. "What do you want your life to look like? How do you want to spend your time? What are you good at? What do you enjoy?"

She put her hands up. "Whoa, whoa, whoa. I'm not looking for you to restructure my life, Tony Robbins."

He laughed. "I'm just saying you shouldn't make decisions on a whim. You should have an end goal in mind. That way – "

"I have lots of goals in mind." She stood and walked over to his work station. He looked comically large, stooping over the little table she'd cleared for him. He always insisted it was comfortable. "Here's a question."

"What?"

"Why do you think Lillian's boyfriend is refusing to visit her?"

Rob shrugged, his bicep within reach again. "What'd he say?"

"He said he's too busy. I can tell Lillian is upset about it, but she doesn't complain. She doesn't want to leave the island yet."

"Maybe he misses her," Rob offered.

"Does he? Because in two weeks he's going on a business trip for a month, and he made it sound like she needed to be back when he returned."

"Maybe, since he travels so much for work, he doesn't like to travel outside of that."

Lucy rolled her eyes. "I'm not buying that either. I know for a fact he has a ton of airline miles. So why not spend some on his girlfriend instead of going to Vegas with his friends?"

"Let me guess," Rob said, taking a deep breath. "You don't like the guy."

"I wouldn't say that. I'm not big on judgment. They've been together for a long time, and it seemed like they were going to get married."

"And you can't stand him."

"No. Honestly, I don't know him. I've only hung out with him a couple of times, you know?"

"I see." Rob nodded, hand on his chin like he was working on a difficult philosophical problem. "Has he always been like this?"

"I don't know. Lillian never complained. She seemed happy – at least from afar. Now that I'm with her all the time, though, she doesn't seem so content."

He flashed a smile. "Here you go again, deciding how people should be happy."

She laughed and lightly shoved him in the shoulder.

Wow, that was a *really* soft shirt. That couldn't be pure cotton. Unless it was some sort of special Egyptian cotton with a different weave...

"I'm just kidding," he said. "I'm not trying to upset you."

"I know." She straightened. No more touching him. "I'd think that if you're on the brink of getting engaged with some-one, you should be bursting with excitement about spending your life with that person. Right? Lillian just doesn't seem that way."

"What does she seem like?"

"I don't know. Sad?"

Rob still had that devilish smile on his face. "Maybe Lillian isn't the bursting type."

"She is," Lucy said firmly. "It seems like she never wants to talk about him. She seems...resigned to marrying him."

"I thought you didn't judge?"

"I'm not judging. It's just what I see, and I'm worried."

Rob thought on this for a moment before responding. "Change is hard for people. We'd much rather slowly ruin our lives than confront our demons."

"Amen." Lucy paused. "Wait, was that directed at me?"

He smiled. "No, you're committed to change. Even to the point where it ruins your life."

She nodded. "Thank you. That's what I thought."

Chapter Twenty-one

It was impossible to sleep that night. The apartment Rob had rented had become as bad as the office, except all of the noise came from within. The radiators rattled, the water heater zipped and whirred, and there was some impossible to find device that beeped every six to eleven hours.

Rob had started having trouble sleeping a few weeks ago, and now the exhaustion was becoming unbearable. He turned and fluffed his pillow, telling himself not to look at his watch. If he looked, he would do the math about how long he'd been lying awake. If he did the math, he'd only become more frustrated and stay awake longer.

He flipped over and pulled the blanket over his shoulder. It wasn't cold, but sometimes making it cozier helped.

Rob laid there, eyes squeezed shut, and started counting. Sometimes if he counted up slowly, he could get himself to fall asleep.

One, two, three...

He got to four hundred before he stopped. It was pointless. The bed was perfectly comfortable, the temperature was fine. The problem was in his head.

The counting couldn't solve the problem of his mind being far too awake. It was like once the lights flipped on, they wouldn't shut off no matter what he did.

Tonight, as with most nights, it was a replay of snippets from the day – things he said, things he wished he'd said. His father, his mother, Claire, Lucy's cruise ship dreams, the chef they'd left in Spain...

It was an erratic, pointless loop, almost manic at times. He tried to redirect his mind.

One, two, three...

Lucy had touched his arm. Had she meant to do it? She was sort of hitting him, not touching exactly. It wasn't done in a nice way, but still. It could be considered flirting in some circles.

That would be...something. His mind spun at the idea. Could Lucy go from despising him to possibly almost liking him? What would it be like to take her on a date? What would it be like to kiss her?

And yet, if she heard about his idea to condemn The Grand Madrona, she wouldn't be flirting with him. She wouldn't pretend to hit him, either. She would probably attack him.

Yet Rick said they'd run into a roadblock. They were supposed to hear the final decision any day, and it didn't look good for OSS. The hotel seemed like it'd be fine. OSS would move onto something else, and Lucy would never know about his stupid plan. She'd never hear about any of it, and maybe she'd take a new job in the city. He could take her to all of his favorite restaurants, and maybe to a comedy show? She'd like that. He was sure of it. He loved the way laughs burst out of her, and how her nose scrunched up when she was thinking hard about something...

Rob switched sides and started over.

One, two, three, four...

He shouldn't have told her all that stuff about his dad. The stories were true, but they were a collection of his dad's worst moments. He wasn't a bad person. He was complicated, like everyone else. A focused man who had achieved a lot in life.

Rob's dad had started with nothing. His own father had abandoned his family when he was young, and he'd stepped up and started working at a factory to help his mom and siblings.

A biographer could tell his story any way they wanted – they could paint him as a man who was a hero, working tirelessly for his family, or as a tyrant who didn't allow imperfection.

In truth, he was both men. He'd given them *everything* growing up, and yes, he expected everything in return. He didn't want his kids to be entitled, so he pushed them to be great.

Was that how Rob's life had ended up here? Preying on the beloved hotel of a woman who had never known happiness?

No, that wasn't what Lucy had said. Claire wasn't unhappy. The hotel had given Claire purpose, as it was the only thing she'd ever done for herself, because she was a saint with no flaws.

Rob sat up. He was spiraling. There is no use trying to force his eyes to stay closed. If he wasn't going to sleep, he might as well get some work done.

He got up from bed, went to his desk, and logged onto his computer.

Four twenty-nine. He'd been awake for three hours. Giving up was the right decision.

His inbox had a decent pile of emails, and Rob got to work answering them. There was a long email chain his boss had forwarded to him with the concerning subject, "We're losing them."

Rob clicked through and skimmed the back and forth. It was between Rick and the guys at Grippy. It seemed the owners of Grippy were getting antsy – they wanted to announce the new development on Orcas at the shareholder's meeting. Rick had responded, telling them not to lose their heads and not to rush things.

Rick wasn't happy, clearly, but Rob was confident he could calm things down at Grippy. He'd been working tirelessly – when he wasn't joking around with Lucy – to find a new location for the Grippy build. He'd also outlined arguments against Orcas Island so they wouldn't feel the sting of what they'd lost.

He talked about how getting to and from the island was inconvenient, and how a large influx of people might be more than the infrastructure could handle. Also, the fact that the county was hostile to developers took the choice out of their hands.

He'd put it all together in a presentation. It wasn't quite done, but it seemed a good time to send it to Rick.

Rob attached it to a new email and hit send. His phone rang six minutes later.

Rick. That guy never slept.

"Morning."

"Glad to see you've got a plan," Rick said.

Rob smiled. "Always."

"Let's get you out to San Francisco. You can present this tomorrow, maybe the day after."

Shoot. He and Lucy had planned to go horseback riding tomorrow. It was Lucy's idea, of course, but it would have to wait. "Sure. No problem."

"I'll have Cherry book your flight. Just get this thing ready. I'll meet you there."

As disappointed as Lucy would be that he'd need a raincheck on the horseback riding, one day he might be able to tell her how close Claire had come to losing the hotel, and maybe she'd forgive him.

But probably not without a lot of yelling.

He could handle it, though. Maybe she'd touch his arm again.

Rob smiled to himself and got up to pack a bag.

Chapter Twenty-two

Try as she might, Lillian was having a hard time hiding that her phone calls with Mason were becoming both more frequent and more heated. Two days ago, Lucy had overheard them arguing about Lillian's return to Texas.

Mason started with his usual arguments. "It stinks. I'm just here waiting around for you to come back and I miss you."

"I miss you too," she said. "But you do realize that's how it is for me when you travel all the time, right?"

He scoffed. "No. This is completely different."

"It really isn't. I wait around for you, and sometimes when you're only back for a week you barely have time to – "

Mason cut her off. "When I travel, it's for work, not for fun. I'm doing it for our future."

"Family is more important than work," Lillian countered. "I hardly ever get to see my mom, and if you came – "

"No, Lil. Don't start with this. You're there by choice. When I go on work trips, it's so I can get promoted and we can buy a house one day."

Lucy shut her eyes. He made plenty of money. He could buy a house tomorrow if he wanted. That was just another one of his recurring arguments. He insisted they needed some million-dollar monstrosity to be happy. "I won't settle for less," he'd say, and normally Lillian would hold her tongue.

But today... "You're making a choice, too. To spend more time at work and less time with both of our families, and with each other."

"Yeah, but it's all for you," he insisted.

It was like talking to a wall. "It's not for me, because I don't care about the money!" she snapped. "I don't need to live in a mansion or have an expensive car. So don't say it's for me when it's not for me."

"Okay. So, what?" he said, voice rising. "Do you expect me to have some regular nine-to-five job where I make, like, ninety thousand dollars a year?"

Lillian didn't know how to respond to that. That was double what she made, and him having a nine-to-five schedule would be great. Incredible, even!

He worked so much and traveled so often that he'd missed weddings, her birthday (more than once), anniversaries, and countless nights in. She could count on one hand the number of times he'd met Lucy and Rose.

She cleared her throat. "Um, yeah, that sounds perfect. Sign up for that, please."

"Don't be ridiculous."

They went back and forth for another half hour, making no progress. Lillian grew tired of keeping her voice low to whisper fight with him, so she finally relented, saying she'd think about coming back to Texas when he returned from his next business trip.

All of her whispering was in vain, however, because she was so fired up that as soon as she got off the phone, she marched right into the living room and told Lucy about the entire conversation.

It was a mistake, but one she couldn't stop herself from making.

Lucy listened intently, and when Lillian was done venting, the questions started.

Lucy couldn't get past the ninety thousand dollar line. "What is that supposed to mean? Does he think that's a bad salary? How much does this guy make?" She paused. "What does he think of *your* salary?"

Lillian rolled her eyes. "He calls anything less than six figures 'peanut money.' "

"Peanut money!" Lucy burst into a laugh, doubling over and holding her stomach. "That's too much."

Lillian, feeling validated, went on. "He says I'm lucky I'm not career-focused like him, so I don't have to worry about these things."

Lucy's mouth popped open. "That's outright condescending. You're great at your job, and it's important. I think you're underpaid, but a lot of important jobs are underpaid."

Mason didn't see it that way. He'd never said as much, but she could tell. In his eyes, people who pursued careers for anything but money were foolish. Suckers, even.

She told herself it was a balance – she could do good in the world and he could focus on finances. Yet somehow, it felt like it wasn't working.

She forced a smile. "Thanks. It's dumb. Just a dumb fight we have all the time."

"It's not dumb," Lucy said. "It's not about money or traveling. It's about him not listening. He's telling you what's important to you, instead of hearing what is actually important to you."

Lillian's stomach sank. "Huh. I've never thought of it that way."

"Not that I'm a relationship expert by any means." Lucy flopped onto the couch. "But he's kidding himself if he thinks you care about him making all this money."

"Yeah." Lillian sat down next to her. "I don't know why he's so stubborn about it."

Lucy nodded but said nothing.

Lillian spoke again. "He really thinks his work is important, so I don't want to take that away from him. It's just...now he's seeing how tough it is for me to be alone all the time. Maybe he'll make an effort to travel less."

"Yeah, maybe."

That was enough talking about herself. How boring she was being. "What about you?"

Lucy turned to her. "What about me?"

"Are you and Rob official yet?"

She made a face. "Officially what?"

Lillian smiled to herself. Lucy always acted like she was above relationships. She could have a full-blown boyfriend for a year and never once refer to him as such.

For years, Lillian didn't understand what that was about. Now she knew, though. It was Lucy's way of trying to head off heartbreak, as though it could be prevented if she just didn't admit she loved the person.

"You know," Lillian said. "Officially dating."

Lucy stood up and walked to the kitchen. "I don't need this from you."

"What!" Lillian laughed. "Oh come on, I told you about Mason. It just seems like..."

"What?"

"Like you and Rob get along well. That's all. He's cute, too. Don't act like you haven't noticed."

Lucy lowered herself so her face was half obscured behind the fruit bowl on the counter. "I'm not blind."

"Maybe you can reschedule your horseback ride for something more romantic."

Lucy stood. "He's a work friend. A sort of colleague."

"What? Because he does his work at the farm shop?"

She shrugged. "Yeah."

Right. Lucy was heavily in denial. For her to make up this colleague line meant that she was too far gone, probably madly in love. "You should ask him out."

"Why?" Lucy made a face. "I'm not – "

"Before someone else does," Lillian added.

A scowl crossed Lucy's face and she stared, chewing the inside of her cheek.

If there was anything Lucy couldn't resi~~tion.~~ The thought of some other chick asking o~~refused~~ to admit she liked?

Infuriating.

Lillian tried not to smile. She wasn't trying to be annoy~~but~~ a little taunting went a long way with Lucy.

Lucy's face moved from a scowl to a blank stare, and just when it looked like Lucy was about to answer, the sound of Lillian's cell phone rang out.

"Hold that thought." She took a deep breath. She didn't want to keep arguing with Mason, but she wasn't going to ignore him either. She pulled the phone out of her pocket. "Oh. It's Mom."

Lucy leaned over. "Oh no. Do you think she's okay?"

"I'm sure she's fine," Lillian said evenly.

Lucy still hadn't gotten over the last hospital scare. It was best to keep her from obsessing.

Before Lillian could think of how to gracefully leave the area, Lucy reached over and tapped on the screen, answering the call and turning on speaker phone.

Lillian let out a sigh. "Hey Mom."

"Hi honey. How are you?"

"I'm good. What's up?"

"Well..." She paused. "We got some bad news at the hotel."

Chip's voice boomed in the background. "Terrible news!"

Lillian looked at Lucy. Her eyes were as wide as a kitten's. "What happened?"

Her mom sighed. "The hotel is going to be condemned."

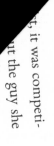

head. "That makes absolutely

We should've taken that guy at

illian.

ed to buy the hotel from me at

"He made a vague threat, like

.... but nothing ever came of it."

"It could be unrelated," Lillian said. "Maybe this was just a mix up in an office somewhere."

"It doesn't feel like a mistake. It feels connected."

Lucy sprung from the couch and started pacing the room. "First the farm, now this?"

"Is that Lucy?"

"Uh, yes," Lillian said. "She's here too. You're on speaker."

"Don't worry," Lucy said, shouting into the phone. "We will fix this."

"I don't want you getting upset," she said. "You've had enough excitement for the month and – "

"Oh no," Lucy said, her voice still too loud. "Don't try to keep me out of it. It's not going to work. When is it being condemned?"

"There's a hearing in two and a half weeks," Chip yelled back.

Lillian shook her head. Surely no one could argue The Grand Madrona Hotel was in such poor condition that it needed to be condemned? It was outside of the realm of possibility.

"Why is it being condemned?" asked Lucy. "Chip, did you cheap out on some important renovations?"

"No!" he said. "Everything is up to code. Everything."

"Then they have no case," Lucy said confidently. "I'll be over in twenty minutes."

Lucy ended the call before anything else could be said.

"Are you coming?" she asked, grabbing her purse from the counter.

This was the sort of thing she had missed out on by living so far away. There was no way she was going to leave now. Maybe when Mason got back from his next month-long assignment this would all be settled and they could get back to normal.

She beamed. "I'm in!"

Chapter Twenty-three

Once at the hotel, Lucy joined Chip in ranting about how ridiculous the notice was, how they had no time to prepare, and also how they were going to bury whoever was behind it.

After half an hour, Lillian interrupted them. "Are you two done?"

Lucy crossed her arms. "For now."

Complaining didn't do anything to help their cause, but it made Lucy feel better. She and Chip took their seats as Claire read the letter about the upcoming vote aloud.

For such a monumental declaration, it didn't say much. It stated the address of One Grand Madrona Drive was to be condemned and utilized for redevelopment. It listed the date of the hearing and provided absolutely no one to contact for questions.

"Unbelievable!" Lucy said once Claire was done. "How can they do this?"

"They can't," Chip said. "We won't let them."

Lillian and Claire exchanged glances. Lucy could feel their worry from across the room, and Claire seemed especially affected. She sat with her shoulders scrunched forward and her head down, as if she were shrinking.

Claire stood and released a shaky breath. "I knew this hotel was too good to be true – and too good to last. Things were going so well. At least we enjoyed it while we had it."

Lucy stared at her. Maybe Claire was flawed after all. She gave in too easily. Not only did she give up on things, she also gave up on herself. Where was her fight? Where was her fury? Lucy would fight to the death over a parking space if it was raining hard enough. Why didn't Claire have that in her for the hotel?

Perhaps it wasn't a true flaw. Lucy knew not everyone could, or should, be like her. A world full of Lucys would be terrifying.

"We're not giving up!" Lucy finally said. She pulled out her phone and started searching online. "Okay, here's something. It looks like the phrase 'redevelopment' is associated with something called eminent domain claims."

"Eminent domain?" Chip shook his head. "What could that possibly have to do with the hotel?"

"Well," Lillian said slowly, "They could have plans to build a hospital, or a highway, or – "

"They're not going to build a highway on Orcas Island." Lucy scoffed. "No. That makes no sense. Why would they pick here?"

Claire shook her head. "I have no idea, but Lillian's right. It could be anything, and it looks like we won't find out for a few weeks."

"Oh, we are not waiting a few weeks," Lucy said. "Who sent this letter?"

"It doesn't say."

"I'm betting the county council knows about this," Chip said. "Claire, isn't Margie's daughter on the council?"

"Who, Tiffany?" Lucy asked. "Tiffany would definitely help us."

"No, not Tiffany, Jade," Claire said. "She's not on the county council exactly, but she worked with them to make that new state park on San Juan."

Lucy nodded. She knew Jade, too, and was sure she'd help. "Perfect. I'll start there. We need to figure out who started this, and then we can figure out how to fight it."

She disappeared into the hallway and started her hunt with a phone call.

"Hey Lucy! It's been so long!"

Lucy winced. Jade had answered cheerfully, so much so that Lucy felt a bit guilty diving right into what she needed.

Not too guilty, though. "I know! I'm sorry, I'm the worst. I'm calling because we're in a crisis over here."

"What's going on?"

She explained the letter and what she knew about the situation. Jade was horrified and promised to do whatever she could. She thought one of the county council members would at least be open to explaining what was happening.

The only problem was that it was Saturday. Jade promised to call her council friend immediately, but she warned they may not have time to talk until later that week. The woman, Angie, owned a restaurant in Roche Harbor and was quite busy on the weekends.

Though she wished it could happen faster, she would play with the hand she was dealt. Lucy said any time would be great and thanked Jade for her help.

They ended the call and Lucy got back to work. First she read a truly horrifying story about a neighborhood claimed by eminent domain. It was supposed to be for a factory – the company claimed it would bring jobs to the area and be a net positive.

In the end, the factory was never built, and hundreds of people had lost their homes.

Horrible.

This led Lucy down a rabbit hole, and she eventually found a grassroots website with a guide on how to survive eminent domain abuse. It was an excellent resource, and she copied down the list of documents they needed to get – everything from ordinances about the island, to proposals for development, to "Vision" plans and studies of the area, and any findings that designated the area as "blighted" or slated for "redevelopment."

According to the guide, she'd likely have to file a Freedom of Information Act request to get most of this stuff.

This slowed her down for about half an hour. Lucy couldn't stop fuming about this fact. She had to draw up a FOIA request to beg for a crumb of information about why her hotel was being taken away without warning?

Ridiculous!

Okay, it wasn't *her* hotel, but it felt that way. The whole situation was absurd, and it only fueled her rage. Lucy wasn't going to let paperwork stop her.

Sunday was spent working on the FOIA request and reaching out to the greater island community to see if anyone knew what was going on. People were supportive, but ultimately no one had heard of this condemnation or of plans to "revitalize" the area where The Grand Madrona stood.

On Monday, Lucy took off work and caught the ferry to San Juan Island to meet with Jade and Angie. The ride over went quickly, with her reading more stories about businesses taken over by eminent domain requests. She was midway through the story of a family farm being seized when she got a call from Rob.

"Hey, I stopped into the farm shop and they said you were out for the day. Is everything okay?"

Oh shoot. She'd completely forgotten he was back in town. "I'm fine, but everything is most definitely not okay."

"What happened?"

Lucy rubbed her face. The sun's reflection on the water was blinding her already tired eyes. "Claire got a letter that the hotel is going to be condemned."

She waited for him to respond, and when there was nothing, she spoke again. "Are you still there?"

"Yeah, yes, I'm here. Sorry. That's shocking."

"Tell me about it. I called off work today. I've got to figure some things out." Silence again. "Rob?"

"I'm here, sorry, just – do you know why it's going to be condemned?"

"I have no idea! I'm on my way to talk to a member of the county council. I'm not sure how much she can tell me, but hopefully more than I know now, which is nothing."

"Oh."

"Don't wait up. I'll be gone all day. How was your trip?"

"It was fine. I'm really sorry about this."

"Don't be sorry, it's not your fault. I have to go. I'll talk to you later."

"Okay, let me know if – "

She accidentally hung up on him while he was still talking.

Whoops. She'd apologize to him later.

The ferry was about to pull in and Lucy got in line to deboard – she wasn't going to waste time stuck behind meandering tourists.

She was the first one off and spotted Jade's car immediately.

"Hey!" Lucy said as she hopped into the passenger's seat. "Thanks again for doing this."

"Any time!" Jade pulled out of her spot and headed toward Roche Harbor. Along the way, she chatted and pointed out landmarks and island highlights.

Even in her fury, Lucy could appreciate Jade's calm demeanor. For a moment, her mind quieted.

It didn't hurt that San Juan was such a pretty island. It shared a lot of similarities to Orcas – the same pastoral charms, the beautiful ocean views. Yet it still had its own distinct feel. There were more people, more businesses, and yes, more tourists – but somehow, it worked.

When they got to Angie's restaurant, Lucy felt so relaxed that she'd been lulled into a bout of sleepiness.

They got out of the car and she told herself to snap out of it. Now wasn't the time to relax. It was a cool, rainy day, normally her favorite napping weather, but not today.

The town of Roche Harbor was adorable, of course. In the center stood a historic hotel called the Hotel de Haro.

It looked classy. Had it ever been targeted by eminent domain developers? Lucy made a mental note to reach out to the owners.

Angie greeted them at the door of her restaurant and led them to an office in the back. It was small and cramped, filled with papers and books, but Angie was welcoming enough. She offered tea and cookies, which only Jade accepted.

Lucy didn't want tea. She jumped right into her interrogations. "Do you know anything about The Grand Madrona Hotel being condemned by the county?"

Angie nodded. "I know a little. I'm not sure how much I'm allowed to share."

Of course. Why would the owners of the hotel deserve to know why they were being condemned? "But it wasn't the council who initiated it?"

Angie shook her head. "Definitely not! We received a request from above, actually. There wasn't anything we could do."

"You're required to hold the hearing?" asked Jade.

"Yes," Angie said. "I do know there was a report declaring the area as blighted."

"That's ridiculous!" Lucy said. "The hotel is in perfect condition. It's never done better! How could it be blighted?"

Angie spun her computer screen to face them. "Here, these are some of the pictures we were sent along with the report about the area."

Lucy leaned forward. She didn't recognize the first picture – it looked like overgrown grass. "That's not the hotel."

Angie clicked through, eventually reaching a picture of the old honey shop and the collapsing barn.

"Oh," Jade said in a low voice. "That doesn't look good."

"It says these structures are abandoned and that they're a fire hazard," Angie said, reading from the screen. "Do you know these places?"

What a joke. How could anyone argue that the hotel had anything to do with this?

Lucy let out a sigh. "Yes, they're near the hotel, but they're not on our property."

Angie frowned. "I'm afraid the hotel may be collateral damage."

Lucy's jaw dropped. "How is that fair!"

"It isn't." Angie spun the screen around again. "Which is why I'm telling you. I could get in trouble for this, so please, don't tell anyone I showed you this report."

This, too, seemed insane to Lucy, but at the same time, made perfect sense. Whoever was coming after them had money and power, and they would use it to silence them. "I understand. I appreciate your help – really."

"I saw what you did for Grindstone Farm. That was incredible." Angie offered a weak smile. "I wish you the best of luck."

"Thank you." Lucy stood from her seat. She'd heard enough. The council didn't have much power in this, but someone did. She had to figure out who that was.

Jade got up and gave Angie a hug. "Thanks again, Angie."

She smiled and nodded. "Of course. You might want to contact the owners of the other properties and see if they're able to make the repairs or demolish the offending structures."

Lucy nodded. "Okay, I can do that."

"Also," Angie dropped her voice, "You didn't hear this from me, but bring the hotel's financials to the hearing. You'll want to prove its usefulness to the community."

Lucy nodded. "Done."

"Great." Angie returned to her normal volume and opened the door to her office. "I assume you've hired an attorney?"

"Almost," Lucy said. "None of the offices were open this weekend, but I'll call today."

"Good. They can work with you from there."

Jade turned to her and smiled. "It seems like you have a good plan, Lucy."

"I hope so."

"I'm sorry this is happening," Angie said. "But I can't tell you anything more, and I can't show bias. So, I guess what I'm saying is – "

"Show up prepared," Lucy said with a nod. "I understand."

"Thanks again for your help!" Jade said.

"Yes." Lucy followed her lead and forced herself to smile like she was on Rob's dad's yacht and her life depended on it. "Thank you so much!"

They parted ways and on the ferry ride back, Lucy managed to schedule video meetings with three attorneys.

They would be ready. She would make sure of it.

Chapter Twenty-four

It didn't sound like Lucy knew he was behind the condemnation of The Grand Madrona. Or at least he was confident she wasn't a skilled enough of an actress to hide it if she did.

That was good. Yet the rest of the situation was bad.

No.

Disastrous.

How had the letters gone out without Rob knowing about it? While he was off in California, selling his heart out to the entire Grippy team, the world had been falling apart behind him.

He left the farm shop and called Rick, who answered right away. "Talk to me, baby."

Way too cheerful. Not a good sign.

"Hey," Rob said. "I thought we were moving past Orcas Island?"

"Business moves fast, baby!"

Rob shut his eyes. That was two baby's in a row. Rick had to be drinking or something.

"How can it move that fast? I just presented to Grippy two days ago. They were happy with our new plans. They liked the alternative sites and – "

"Yeah, but then we got approval to move forward with our revitalization plan for Orcas Island. The letters were overnighted to the property owners. Didn't Cherry tell you?"

Oh, Cherry. Rick's ever-negligent secretary. "She failed to mention it."

"Then I'll break the good news to you: we got lucky. It turns out we have a friend out there."

"What kind of a friend?"

"A judge. Don't worry about it; just focus on securing the condemned status. We've basically got it in the bag."

This was not happening. Rob needed to take a seat. "I don't know, Rick. There are a lot of reasons to push Grippy to another location. After I looked at the – "

Rick cut him off. "No. They liked your other ideas, but nothing beats that island. They were thrilled when I told them our eminent domain should go through. I heard they announced it at their shareholder meeting this morning."

Rob's stomach dropped. "They did *what?* They shouldn't be sharing that with anyone yet."

"Rob, Rob, since when do you worry so much? They're excited! That's good for us. They had the mockups on display like proud new parents. It's all anyone can talk about."

Nausea washed over him and he wrestled his suit jacket off before unlocking his car and getting into the driver's seat.

This was all moving too fast. Why was Rick so confident they'd be able to pull this off? He was setting Grippy up for disappointment. Not only that, but OSS would look like amateurs if they failed now.

Rick was still babbling on. "I'm sending over a few things you need to do before the hearing, got it?"

Rob stared straight ahead. How was he going to stop this out of control train?

"You can handle this, right?" Rick let out a sigh. "Tell me you can handle this."

Rob let out a long breath. "I can handle this."

"Good."

The line went dead and Rob sat in his car for the next half hour, running over everything in his head.

There was still a chance it wouldn't go through, right? Rick was always confident, overconfident even.

Maybe Rob could talk to Grippy again and convince them to change to one of the alternate sites he'd proposed. The mockups could essentially stay the same, but they could save money on the location.

No, that argument wouldn't work. They knew they'd get the land on Orcas at a bargain. It was incomparable. They'd offer pennies and the landowners would have no choice but to accept.

It was robbery, really. Not that he'd ever thought of it like that before...

He needed to see what the team at OSS had put together. Had the eminent domain team made *that* strong of a case? Or was the judge just crooked? Paid off? A dunce?

Yeah, that could be it.

Rob started his car and drove over to his office. As promised, Rick had sent over hundreds of pages of documents and arrangements.

The smell of fried seafood was as unbearable as ever and the music pounded through the walls, but this time it had no effect on him. Rob was determined. He settled into his desk and spent the next three hours poring over every detail.

It seemed like the eminent domain team had been active behind the scenes. They'd hired a team of surveyors, analysts, and economists. Each specialist had written a report after report highlighting how badly the area was doing.

They struck every imaginable point – decreased value of the surrounding home prices due to the overgrown lots, fire risk from the old buildings, loss of tourism and tax revenue from underutilized properties.

These were all significant to the county, and as much as he hated to admit it, it was a productive argument for seizing the land. Rob could almost kick himself for coming up with the idea in the first place.

By the end of the day, he had to strain to keep his eyes open, but he couldn't stop reading. He needed to find a solution that would make everyone happy.

He was engrossed in stacks of reports when the door to his office flew open.

"This is a nightmare!"

It was Lucy.

He stared up at her like a mouse caught in a trap.

"You don't look so good." She sat down in the chair opposite his desk. "Are you okay?"

"Yeah. Sorry." He shuffled the papers so they were hidden behind his computer. "It's been a long day."

"Me too." She paused. "But tell me about your day first."

He shook his head. "It's nothing interesting. What have you been up to?"

She threw her hands up. "Everything! Claire and I just hired an attorney. We're meeting with him tomorrow."

"What kind of attorney?"

"He specializes in eminent domain takeovers." Lucy dropped the words stiffly, as if they were sharp on her tongue. "He says we have a tough case ahead of us."

Rob winced. "Really?"

"I have confidence, though. The community will be behind us on this one."

His hands were getting clammy. He slipped them under the desk so she wouldn't see. "Any idea what they're planning to develop? You know, in case the community likes that too?"

She bit her lip. "Good point. Hopefully it's something dumb like a waste management plant, and not something shiny and exciting like...I don't know, a waterpark."

"You're right." He cracked a smile. "The residents have been clamoring for a waterpark."

Lucy let out a laugh. "Whatever it is, we'll be ready."

He needed to tell her the truth. She deserved to know what he'd done. If she found out from someone else, she would never forgive him.

She still might never forgive him, but...

"What?" She leaned forward. "Don't you believe me?"

He jolted out of his thoughts. He didn't need to tell her yet. He could still fix it. "I believe you. I always believe in you. That's what scares me."

She threw her head back and cackled maniacally. "Sorry," she said after a moment. "I'm a bit off kilter."

"More so than with the farm?"

"Of course. This is personal." She paused, staring into his eyes. "You know, now would be the time to do something nice for me."

He sputtered out a laugh. "I'm sorry?"

She nodded. "You heard me."

His mouth had gone totally dry. She knew. She must know. Why else would she say something like that? She was waiting to see if he confessed and he didn't. Now –

"You ruined my horseback ride," she said, leaning forward, "and now I'm going to be stressed about the hotel for two weeks. I could use something nice."

His heart pulled the throbbing lump out of his throat. "What were you thinking?"

She shrugged and stood up. "I don't know. Think about it and get back to me."

She walked out of the office and left Rob sitting there with his mouth hanging open.

He was in trouble, and in more ways than one.

Chapter Twenty-five

Was that too forward?

Lucy got to her car and the doubts started flooding in. Rob had seemed caught off guard by what she'd said.

But she couldn't help herself! All of this business with the hotel had her in a tizzy. Lucy felt wild, out of control. Plus, Lillian's teasing had been echoing in her mind, and something just snapped.

Maybe she liked Rob, maybe she didn't. How else would she know if she didn't force him to take her out?

It was entirely possible he didn't like her. That was fine. She could deal with that. Rejection was nothing new to Lucy.

Rejection was better than him being scared of her. He wouldn't be the first guy she'd scared off, but for him to act all tough and cool and then panic the *one* time she demanded to be taken out?

Pathetic.

Thankfully, he called her later that night and asked when she'd be free for dinner and "an activity."

"I'm not sure. Maybe Saturday? It's hard to get work done on Saturday nights because no one else is working."

"I hear you," he said. "Okay, I've got a plan. Be ready at three thirty?"

Lucy raised an eyebrow. "What if three thirty isn't good for me?"

"Then tell me and we can change it."

Lucy frowned. She had no problem with three thirty. It was a reflex to challenge him. They'd never been a "we" before, and she wasn't sure if she liked it. "No," she finally said. "Three thirty is good."

They ended their call and Lucy got back to work. She was making progress, but she'd feel better once they had their attorney picked out and the FOIA request came back with documents detailing why this was happening. The whole situation was bizarre – why was it so hard to find out why they were being condemned, and by whom?

She did what she could, however, and day by day, she got closer to the truth. All week, Lucy couldn't help but think how nice it was having something to look forward to. Even if her date with Rob was just a distraction, it was helpful. It pulled her out of her manic state every now and then.

By the end of the week, their fabulous and wildly expensive attorney took over most of the paperwork. That was a relief. Paperwork wasn't Lucy's forte.

That gave them more time to focus on other tasks. They decided to divide and conquer – each person had their own strengths. Even Aunt Becca made the trip up to Orcas to try to help. Just her being there seemed to lift Claire's spirits.

Marty worked on building a website with news, updates, and ways for people in the community to help.

Lillian partnered with Jade to garner community support. They created a petition to save the hotel and surrounding properties. They'd collected nearly eight hundred signatures so far. For such a small county, that was a lot, and the number grew daily.

Lucy met up with her contact at the local paper. They were happy to run an article about the mysterious slew of proposed condemnations, and added a link to Marty's website at the bottom.

Of everyone, Chip ended up becoming the MVP. He managed to get a hold of everyone who owned land near the hotel. There were several other properties that were slated to be condemned, and some of the owners hadn't even known, since they so rarely visited or checked their mail.

This proved to be a positive. Chip was able to convince them to give him the freedom to tidy up their land, even going as far as demolishing decaying buildings.

"They weren't happy about it," he said. "But it beats losing the land altogether."

From there, he hired a team of contractors and landscapers to clear out brush and make it look as though each parcel was "responsibly owned."

It was all coming together nicely. Lucy was still worried about the situation, but it felt good to have a team in place.

By the time Saturday rolled around, Lucy felt relaxed enough to spend an embarrassingly long time planning what to wear on her night out with Rob.

In some misguided attempt at being mysterious, he wouldn't tell her where they were going. All he said was to dress warm, but to not wear farm clothes.

As if she owned farm clothes.

Lucy erred on the side of elegance, hoping he'd take her somewhere nice, but not too nice. She'd decided to wear a long-sleeved sage colored dress and a knee-length flowing cardigan. She added heels – only three inches, nothing crazy – and Lillian braided half of her hair in a half up, half down look. It was casual, not too try-hard, and even a bit whimsical as little pieces fell out.

Rob picked her up promptly at three thirty and she was relieved to see he was dressed casually – for him, at least. No suit. Just a white button-down shirt, a navy sports coat and a pair of rust colored chinos.

As she got into his car, she announced, "I hope you weren't planning on taking me to ride a horse in this outfit."

"No. Not a horse." He laughed. "A plane."

She snapped her head toward him. "A plane?"

"Just kidding." He recoiled, as if waiting to be struck.

She let out a huff and crossed her arms.

"I booked dinner and a private tour," he said.

"A tour of what?"

"The islands."

"But not on a plane, right? I don't fly."

"I know," he said innocently. "It's on a boat. A sailboat."

"Oh." That didn't sound so bad. She turned to look out the window. Perhaps she should have worn pants, though. Boats were windy, it was still quite cold and her sweater was more of an accessory than something to keep her warm.

Oh well. "That sounds nice."

He smiled, eyes fixed on the road ahead of them.

They drove to Deer Harbor and Lucy spotted their ship as soon as they descended the dock. It stuck out amongst the fishing boats and small yachts, its gleaming white hull glistening in the sun.

It didn't look like a modern sailboat, but more like something out of a pirate movie. It had to be at least a hundred feet long, with two enormous wooden masts standing vertically at either end.

The canvas sails were folded down, and everything, from the floor to the bannisters to the lifeboats, was outlined with brilliant, shining wood.

When they got closer, she could see the spoked wheel at the head of the ship.

She jabbed Rob in the side. "Do you think that's real?"

"The ship?"

"No, that!" she whispered, pointing as subtly as she could. "The steering wheel."

They got into line behind two other couples waiting to board. "Yes. It's called the helm."

She wagged a finger at him. "Ah, right. You're a yacht boy. You know all the official names of things."

"I'm just getting you ready for your next career," he said.

She laughed, and a man in a blue and white captain's hat waved them forward. "Come on, come on. Don't be shy! I'm Captain Kurt. I'll be the one guiding you tonight."

He turned and grabbed two long flutes of champagne, handing one to each of them.

"Nice to meet you," Rob said.

"I like your hat," Lucy added.

Captain Kurt beamed. "Thank you! Come on board, take a look around, and find your table. You can place your dinner order with a member of our fine staff downstairs."

They nodded and walked onto the ship.

"Oh la la," Lucy said, peering at the menu Rob had picked up. "Where should we go first?"

"Anywhere you like."

They strolled the length of the deck, sipping on champagne as Lucy peered over the side every few feet. "It's further down than I thought. Every time I look, it seems like the water is further away than the last time."

"Were you considering making an escape?"

She shrugged. "It's never a bad idea to have an exit in mind."

"Fair point," he said, shaking his head. "Though the water is a little cold."

"That won't stop me," she said confidently, trying to ignore the goosebumps on her arms and legs.

He paused, gazing at her for a moment too long before breaking a smile and saying, "I know. Nothing stops you, does it?"

Lucy's heart jumped and she looked away, over the water. "It's getting chilly. Maybe we should check out the downstairs?"

"Sure."

They crossed the deck and descended a short flight of stairs into a cozy little room. A wall-to-wall lush red carpet softened their footsteps. Scattered around were six small tables, each one topped with a candle and wine glasses. Three of the other couples were already seated, talking in hushed tones.

They took a seat at a table near a rounded window. Lucy made her dinner choice by closing her eyes and pointing at the menu. Rob checked off their choices and handed their menu to a passing waiter.

Then he turned to look at her through the candlelight.

This was a lot. Far more romantic than she'd imagined. The intimacy of it made her feel like she had to make a joke. "You know, Rob, if I didn't know any better, I'd say you were trying to trick me."

"Trick you?" At that moment, he knocked his elbow into the table and sent an empty wine glass flying to the ground.

"Sorry," he said, stooping to collect it. The glass had landed on the carpet and luckily hadn't broken.

After recovering it, Rob sat down, cheeks pink.

Such an easy blusher.

Lucy dropped her voice. "Try not to embarrass me here, Rob."

He burst into a laugh. "I'm doing my best."

A waiter stopped by to fill their wine glasses and drop off an appetizer – calamari with cocktail sauce. Lucy loved it, and even Rob managed to get the food into his mouth without making a mess.

The ship slowly moved out of the dock, and they had a beautiful view from the window. It was so beautiful that Rob couldn't seem to look away, or come up with much to talk about.

"I'm glad we can be inside," Lucy announced as their caprese salads arrived.

He smiled at her briefly before turning back to the window. "Me too."

"How was work this week?" she asked.

"Not great, to be honest."

Maybe that was why he was being so quiet. "I'm sorry. Are you going to get fired?"

"Nah." Rob shrugged. "How's your hotel rescue going?"

"Fine, I guess." She sat back and let out a sigh. "They hardly need me."

"What?" A smile danced on his lips. "Impossible."

She took a bite of her salad. "It's true. We've got an attorney, contractors, landscapers, real estate agents, grannies from all of the islands vowing to start letter writing campaigns..."

"Not the grannies!"

"I know!"

"I wish I could help."

She shook her head. "Please. There's nothing left to do. We're still waiting on our FOIA request. That'll be big."

"When do you expect to get it?"

"They didn't say. Could be any day, could be months."

The waiter dropped off their entrees – Rob had gotten a roasted chicken breast with au gratin potatoes and Lucy's blind pick resulted in a duck confit on a bed of puréed butternut squash.

They ate, and she babbled on about the issues they were having with the county, tearing down the old structures, and tidying up the overgrown lots.

Rob listened dutifully, but after not too long she had the distinct feeling she was talking too much.

"I'm sorry. I'm sure you're sick of hearing about this."

"Not at all." He set his fork down. "I just – ah, have nothing to add."

"We should talk about something else." She paused, jerking her head to a couple on the other side of the room. "I wonder what they're talking about."

"Oh, them?" Rob leaned in and dropped his voice. "Well, he just told her he's sick of her mother."

Lucy raised an eyebrow. "Did he?"

He nodded. "And she said he was welcome to move out and take his snakeskin vest with him."

Lucy chortled a laugh and covered her mouth. "No she did not."

Rob shrugged. "You think I'd lie about that?"

"What about those two?" she said quietly.

He followed her eyes to the couple nearest to them and let out a heavy sigh. "You don't want to know."

She leaned in. "Tell me."

He got closer, his voice almost a whisper. "He said he's sick of her ironing his underwear and it has to stop."

Lucy launched back into her chair, laughing so hard she started to cough and Rob offered her some water. He had an entirely too pleased look on his face.

A moment later, the waiter dropped off their desserts – slices of French silk pie – and they took a break from their people watching to dig in.

Lucy was stuffed, but the pie was so heavenly that she finished it all within minutes.

"How about after you're done, we go back out on the deck?" she suggested.

"I don't want you to be cold."

She felt like she'd eaten enough to keep her warm. "I'm fine. The others are going to take all the good spots if we don't hurry."

He threw his fork onto the table with a clatter. "You're right. Let's go."

Lucy led the way upstairs with Rob following behind. As soon as they reached the deck, the wind hit her and sent a chill through her body.

She was turning to make a comment when they almost bumped heads.

"Sorry," she said, pulling away.

Rob was holding out his sport coat. "I thought you'd need this."

She shook her head. "I have a sweater."

"It's barely anything," he said, stepping forward and draping his coat over her shoulders.

It was much warmer this way, and she decided not to protest. After all, he had those muscles to keep him warm.

They walked to the rear of the ship and found it deserted, the enormous sails now open overhead.

Lucy leaned against the railing, pulling Rob's coat tighter. The sun was setting, reflecting brilliant pink and orange beams off the water.

"You've sort of outdone yourself," she finally said, turning to face him.

A smile crossed his face for a brief moment before fading. "I'm glad you think so. Maybe you'll consider going out with me again?"

Her heart leapt and she paused, pretending to think on it.

It was odd. Lucy's romances never started out this way. It was never slow. Men either recoiled from her immediately, disqualifying themselves as romantic partners, or they pursued her with an intensity that matched her own.

Those tended to fizzle out quickly, though sometimes she'd let it drag out when she couldn't decide how she felt about the guy.

There was no question here. Her heart was pounding in her chest. Somehow, Rob had snuck up on her. He'd worked his way into her life, and now she couldn't imagine him leaving.

"Yeah," she finally said, suppressing a smile. "I think I could do that."

"Lucy..." He looked out onto the water, then back at her. "I've been meaning to tell you something, but I don't know how to do it."

She studied him and squinted her eyes. "Is it going to ruin the moment?"

He took a step closer. "Well, yes, but – "

"Then don't say it." Wearing heels was the right idea. They put her at the perfect height. She leaned in, lifting her face to his.

Rob smiled before leaning down to kiss her.

Chapter Twenty-six

There had to be a way to build Grippy's compound without involving The Grand Madrona hotel. Rob just needed more time to figure it out.

When he got back from his dinner with Lucy, he spent the rest of the night trying to see the problem from every angle. There was a chance they could skip the hotel and instead expand further north or south, though both directions bordered elaborate homes that would be difficult to claim.

After a few hours, he got the wild idea of building the compound over the water of East Sound. From what he could tell online, it was only ninety feet deep.

That didn't sound so bad. Buildings were more than ninety feet high, right? What was a few ninety-foot cement pillars in the grand scheme of things? That'd be something for Grippy to brag about – having an ocean compound.

Unfortunately, after hours of brainstorming, that was his least insane idea. He felt like he was being driven to madness. He couldn't allow the hotel to be taken, and he couldn't allow the deal to fall through, either. There had to be a solution, and he needed it *now*.

It was the madness that almost made him spill his guts to Lucy. The guilt over the project was killing him, and he wanted to throw himself at her mercy. Plus, if anyone would have an idea of what to do, it would be her. But she'd looked up at him with that excitement in her eyes, her hair blowing in the breeze, and that dress...

He couldn't do it. He couldn't tell her. Not only that, she'd told him not to ruin the moment!

Rob knew he was running out of time, but he couldn't lose everything now. She was finally starting to like him.

After their date, he decided what he really needed was to take a page out of Lucy's book. She never let anything stop her. He would find a way to make everyone happy – Grippy, OSS, and Lucy – even if it killed him.

On Sunday, he was busy researching other properties near the hotel when his dad called.

It wasn't a good time to talk, but he so rarely called that Rob didn't dare miss it. "Hey Dad. Everything okay?"

"Yeah, sure."

"Things are hectic at work for me right now."

"That's why I'm calling!" he said with a laugh. "I wanted to congratulate you. I heard about this new deal from your brother. All the Silicon Valley startup guys are going crazy for it. They're saying they need to hire you."

"Oh?" More publicity. Great.

"Don't sound so excited."

"I am excited." Rob leaned back in his chair and closed his eyes. They ached from staring at his computer screen for so long. "It's just been a lot."

"Try not to lose your nerve at the last minute," his dad said. "Don't sabotage yourself. You've done it before, and I can tell you're thinking of doing it again."

Rob sat up. How did his dad know that? "Thanks for the confidence, Dad."

His dad bellowed another laugh. "Be strict with yourself, that's all. Get back to work."

"Will do. See you."

It was perhaps the proudest his dad had sounded in recent years, so of *course* it had to be about this disastrous deal.

How had his dad known he was thinking of ways to back out? Could he hear it in his voice? Or did he have so little faith in him?

Was it really about Lucy? Or was it Rob being weak, again, and thwarting his own success?

Unlike other deals that had fallen through, all he had to do this time was stay out of the way.

Why did it feel impossible?

With his dad's comments rolling around in his head, Rob's insomnia only worsened. By the time Monday rolled around, he was no closer to a solution and as erratic and panicked as ever.

The more tired he got, the more difficult it was to focus. Lucy's face kept flashing into his mind, ripping him away from whatever revenue statements, building proposals, or condemnation arguments he was looking through.

He decided to drop by the farm shop to see Lucy, telling himself it wouldn't hurt his productivity in the least. It would help his inspiration and clarity, and it had absolutely nothing to do with him wanting to see her again.

When he got to the shop, he opened the door and smacked into a towering bookshelf.

"I'm sorry," he said, peering around the corner.

"Oh good!" Lucy popped her head out from behind. "You can help me move this."

He eyed the stack of candles teetering dangerously off one of the shelves. "Should we take all the stuff off first?"

Lucy shook her head. "Absolutely not. That'll take forever. Come on!"

He did as he was told, pushing the shelf as Lucy pulled and steered. She was impressively strong, and they ended up only losing one candle. It hit the floor, bouncing and rolling without a crack.

Once they had the bookshelf where she wanted it, Lucy ran to the other side of the store to rearrange a display of local candy, then to another shelf to move postcards, and finally back to her computer.

"Having a good day, then?" he asked.

"No." She slumped into her chair behind the counter. "I feel useless. There's nothing for me to do here, and there's nothing for me to do for the hotel."

"Maybe that's a good thing," he said. "Maybe you should move on from the hotel."

Lucy clicked away on her laptop. "Yeah right. Move on to what? It's the most important event of our – wait!"

"What?"

"I just got an email! My FOIA request is ready!"

His heart sank. Without realizing it, Rob had started slowly backing up. "I'll let you get to it then."

She ignored him, clicking fiercely. "Oh my gosh. This has three hundred pages of documents."

"Oh yeah?" Could she hear him breathing heavily? It seemed like he was breathing heavily all of a sudden.

"They're trying to bury me in paperwork," she said with a scoff. "It's not going to work! I happen to be excellent with sorting through garbage."

Rob was halfway to the door when he heard Lucy gasp. "What's wrong?" he asked, even though he knew. He knew exactly what was wrong. He needed to run.

"It looks like there's a document about who requested the hotel be condemned. Hang on, it's loading."

What if he just turned and ran out the door? It would give her enough time to process what she was seeing, and it would give him a chance to get to the safety of his car.

But Rob didn't run. He didn't move at all, instead standing there, frozen, staring at her.

He watched as her eyes scanned left to right, left to right. She put a hand on the counter to steady herself before looking up at him.

He cleared his throat. "Is everything okay?" His voice sounded weak, like all the air had gone out of his lungs.

She looked like she was about to speak, but then she stopped, instead getting up and silently walking toward him.

Rob took a step back. "Lucy?"

"I cannot believe you." Her voice was barely above a whisper. She stood in front of him with her fists balled at her sides. "It was you all along."

Rob put his hands up. "It's not what you think it is."

"Isn't it?" Her nostrils flared, her voice growing louder with every word. "Because it *seems* like you've been distracting me for the past few weeks while you were plotting to steal Claire's hotel!"

"That's not what happened. I tried to steer OSS *away* from the hotel. I just did an entire presentation about alternate sites and – "

"When were you planning on telling me you were behind this?"

He looked down, then back up at her. "I wanted to tell you on Saturday, but – "

"But you're a coward and all you care about is your stupid career that doesn't matter?"

He stopped. She had no idea what she was talking about. Who was she to say his career didn't matter? Or to call him a coward, when he'd dedicated so many hours to fixing this? "That's not fair."

"Your entire company is a leech on society."

He drew in a sharp breath and narrowed his eyes. "Am I a leech, too, then?"

"Yeah!" she yelled. "You're the fattest leech of them all!"

Right. He was a leech. So much for her starting to like him. Apparently that was an illusion. "How would you even understand the value of a career when you can't stay in one place for more than six months?"

"I've had plenty of careers! I'm not afraid to walk away if a company wants to do something immoral. You, however, have no qualms. All you care about is money. And yourself."

"Yeah, I only care about myself, but you *really* cared about the farm."

She glared at him. "I did. I do."

"No, you don't. You're just looking for distractions. That's all it was for you, a distraction, and you go from one distraction to the next. You can't commit to a career because you're afraid to put roots down, and you would never understand the sacrifices I've – "

"Get out." She pointed to the door.

He closed his eyes for a moment. He'd gone too far.

The regret hit him instantly. Rob hadn't meant to say it like that. He'd put a lot of thought into Lucy's career troubles, and he naively believed he could be helpful, or insightful. He'd planned to talk to her about it some time, thinking he could help her. He wanted to do it in a way that would show her he'd been thinking about her and that he cared.

Instead, he'd thrown it in her face. "Lucy, please, let me – "

"Good luck at the hearing," she said, pulling the door open and waving a hand for him to go through.

A customer appeared then, at that perfectly awkward moment in time, and tried to make his way around them.

Rob stepped outside to get out of the way. He wanted to take back what he'd said and tell her how sorry he was, but he couldn't form the words, and in his hesitation, she slammed the door in his face.

He stood there, staring ahead, trying to rewind the last five minutes in his mind. It had all fallen apart so quickly, and so spectacularly.

Surely she would forgive him? He told himself if he gave her some time, they could talk it over, work it out.

He made the slow walk to his car, unable to convince even himself that there was any chance of that happening.

Chapter Twenty-seven

What a scoundrel – no, what a *creep!* Lucy had never been fooled so badly in all her life!

Not that she was ready to concede she'd been fooled. She had never liked Rob. Not really.

Sure, she kissed him *once.* Big deal. Deep down, she'd known there was something off about him. She could feel it, and she'd kept him at arm's length until just recently.

If only she'd trusted her gut.

By that evening, she felt like she'd calmed down enough to talk about it. She got home, printed the FOIA documents, and slapped them onto the kitchen table.

Lillian looked up at her, eyes wide. "Is this bad news?"

"You tell me," she said, arms crossed.

Okay, she was still a little angry, but how couldn't she be? She'd been completely swindled and then insulted by an over-grown rich kid!

Lucy watched as Lillian flipped through the documents. When she reached the one detailing how OSS had initiated the request, she looked up with a concerned look on her face. "What did Rob say about this?"

Lucy scoffed. "A bunch of lies. You know how he is."

"Lucy," she said in a low voice. "He must have an explanation for himself."

"He acted like it was the company's doing and not his, but I don't believe him."

Lillian frowned and set the papers aside. "I'm really sorry. I know you liked him."

"I never liked him," she snapped. "He managed to distract me with a cool boat ride, but I wouldn't say I ever liked him."

Lucy cringed when she realized what she'd said. *Distracted.* Apparently, that was what Rob thought she was looking for all along – just another distraction.

He'd provided one, too. He served as the distraction, trying to keep her away from the hotel. It hadn't worked, though. She was as on top of things as ever.

Did he really think he was *so* handsome and *so* smart and *oh so* fun that she'd forget about helping Claire?

The arrogance. He was a cruel person. Cutthroat. All he cared about was work, and he'd do anything to win.

None of that mattered. Lucy wasn't going to let him win. She was going to destroy him.

Until the hearing, Lucy had one focus: doing everything possible to save the hotel from being condemned. She thought their chances looked great.

Okay, not great – that was what she would tell Claire to bolster her spirits – but at the very least, things looked good.

Even their ever-serious lawyer thought so. Their presentation about the hotel was strong, supported by actual numbers and figures. They'd gotten over two thousand signatures from county residents, and on top of that, many islanders pledged to come to the hearing to show their support.

With help, Chip made amazing progress on the shabbier properties, removing the dangerous structures and taming the overgrown lots. It was a miraculous transformation.

Still, even Lucy couldn't gloss over the fact that the other property owners weren't going to suddenly create profitable, taxable businesses. Most of them could barely make it to the hearing.

On the other hand, why did every square inch of land need to make money? The county council couldn't be filled with a bunch of Robs, could it?

Even if the council members preferred to see the land developed, it wasn't that simple. Building the monstrosity that OSS and Grippy wanted wouldn't just bring tax revenue, it would bring people – hundreds of them. Maybe thousands! These people would need somewhere to live, places to eat, places to park their cars – everything!

Some, like Rob, might argue it would be good for the local businesses, but what about the residents in general? How much extra traffic could little Orcas Island sustain?

These arguments rolled around in Lucy's head day and night. In one moment, she could be convinced they were absolutely going to win at the hearing, and an hour later, she could be drenched in despair, thinking they didn't stand a chance.

It was a relief when the day of the hearing finally arrived. Lucy piled on to the ferry with the A-team: Claire, Aunt Becca, Lillian, Chip, and Marty. It was nice being together, and it helped ease some of the tension that had built up over the long days and sleepless nights.

The stress was real. Lucy had never seen Claire so pale and quiet. Claire was in even worse shape than when the FBI was convinced she was harboring a criminal – Marty – and Lucy had ended up in federal prison.

That had been bad, but at least it had passed quickly. It felt like Lucy had been forcing herself to smile and insist things would be okay for months. It was exhausting, especially when she wasn't so certain herself.

On the plus side, their lawyer had prepared them for what to expect during the hearing. He'd be there too, of course, and he warned they should not be intimidated by the large team of lawyers OSS would likely deploy.

He also said there may be crowds protesting for either side, and to try not to get caught up in it.

Lillian reminded Lucy of this fact as the ferry pulled into Friday Harbor. "This means you," she said, eyebrows raised. "No heckling, and no fights."

Lucy let out a laugh. "I know."

"If you do end up in a fight," Aunt Becca added, "tag me in. I'm scrappier than I look."

Lillian shook her head. "Don't encourage her."

"I'm just being supportive!" Aunt Becca added, hands innocently up in the air.

Lucy just laughed. She wasn't afraid of an angry crowd, or a bunch of pushy lawyers. None of that was going to goad her into a fight.

There was only one person she wasn't sure she could handle: Rob.

The thought of him standing there, all cool and detached in one of his stupid suits, made her feel queasy. She didn't know if she could look him in the eye, and that frightened her most of all.

They arrived at the legislative building to find a crowd of at least sixty people outside. Lucy thought that was impressive for ten in the morning on a Thursday – a lazy meeting time if she had ever known one – but it wasn't until they went inside that her breath was taken away. Every single seat was filled, and each wall had bodies crammed against them, pressed close together.

Though the occupancy posted was for forty-nine people, there had to be at least twice that inside.

They spotted Claire's friend Margie running to and fro, directing people and handing out signs. She rushed over to greet them. "You made it! There are six seats at the front, but maybe I can find one more chair so you can all sit together."

"Thanks Margie," Claire said in a small voice.

Margie took one look at her before pulling her in for a hug. "How are you feeling? It's going to be okay," she said, giving Claire no time to respond. "Everyone here is behind you. They saw the news story. It's been the talk of the town! We've been so upset!"

Lucy looked at all of the people who had taken the time out of their day to support them. Some were regulars at the farm shop. Behind them were all of her coworkers from the farm – they must've shut down for the day. Jade was in the back with a gaggle of people, and there were countless other faces she didn't recognize.

She wanted to say something, but when she opened her mouth to speak, her voice caught in her throat and tears welled in her eyes.

This was the community she'd been missing all of her life. These people were there for each other through thick and thin. Even if they didn't agree on everything, they still supported one another. It was something Lucy hadn't truly understood until this moment.

At Margie's prompting, they took their seats up front. Their lawyer greeted them cheerfully before going over some last-minute details in hushed tones.

Lucy had a hard time focusing on what he was saying. She kept looking over her shoulder, afraid she might catch a glimpse of Rob, his broad shoulders and devilish smile taunting her from across the room.

There was no sign of him yet, though, and no one from his side at all. By ten fifteen, the head councilman announced they were done waiting and would start the hearing with the land owner's side of the argument.

Claire and Chip got up, their presentation projected onto a far screen. Marty had put it together for them, complete with pictures, financials, and easy to read arguments.

Lucy and Lillian had helped him cut it down to time, but overall, he was remarkably good at preparing information in this way. Lucy was surprised. Apparently he did do something at that job of his.

Claire spoke first, and Lucy could hardly breathe. She came across well – perhaps a bit humble, but sweet, which was apt, because she was sweet.

It wasn't long before Chip took over. He was a born public speaker, peppering in jokes and rolling laughter over the room. He was the perfect contrast to Claire's modesty, reiterating how great the hotel was, talking about how far they'd come, and what an important part of the community they were.

Their presentation lasted twenty minutes, including five minutes to show the tax revenue and jobs generated by the hotel. It was immediately followed by short talks from the other property owners.

They weren't as polished, but they spoke well and showed pictures of how lovely their lots now looked. Lucy thought no one could argue these places should be condemned.

Or at least, so she hoped. Their side of the argument was done by eleven, and then the council members asked one question each.

Lucy couldn't decide if it was a good sign they didn't have many questions, or a signal that they'd already made up their minds.

Once that was done, the head councilman asked if there was anyone from OSS to represent the condemnation case.

There were a few murmurs from the crowd, but no one stepped forward.

He shook his head. "It seems OSS doesn't think this project is important enough for their presence. We're going to take a brief recess, and if they haven't appeared by then, the council will issue their verdict."

He stood and the room erupted into a chorus of voices. Lucy was startled at first, thinking that perhaps Rob and his demolition crew had finally made their grand entrance, but when she turned around, there was no one. OSS' table sat empty, their side still unrepresented.

After a short fifteen-minute wait, the council returned. The head councilman tapped his microphone and cleared his throat. "Thanks to everyone for coming out today. I'm pretty sure if I don't get you out of here in a few minutes, the fire marshal is going to throw me in jail."

A few chuckles.

He continued. "I will get to the point. This request was a large one, and one we didn't take lightly. The proposed development on Orcas Island would bring substantial revenue and tourism to our county."

There was a rumble of boos from the crowd. Lucy gripped onto the sides of her plastic chair.

"However," he said, his voice booming and silencing them, "the inability of OSS to show even the slightest courtesy in explaining their plans does not inspire confidence. The properties are under good repair, and The Grand Madrona Hotel is a historic and fast-growing business. The request for condemnation has been denied."

Lillian leapt from her seat with a yell before Lucy managed to process what she'd just heard. After a moment, she too stood, grabbing Claire, Aunt Becca, and Lillian into a hug.

The nightmare was finally over.

Chapter Twenty-eight

The livestream of the council meeting kept cutting in and out, but the final message came through loud and clear: the eminent domain request was dismissed, and OSS had lost their bid.

Rob let out a sigh and released the tension from his shoulders. Even with the signal booster he'd brought for himself, it was hard to get a signal out at sea. He tucked his phone into his pocket and opened the door to the ship's bathroom.

Above board, the lawyers were flipping out.

"Did you get in contact with them?" one of them demanded. "Did you tell them we're on our way?"

Rob frowned and shook his head. "I couldn't get through. No one was answering."

"This is ridiculous," said one of the women. "They'll have to reschedule for another day."

Rob nodded. "Absolutely."

He knew there was no chance of that happening. His scheme had worked just as he planned. When Rick told him to get their team of lawyers, field experts, and surveyors to the council meeting on time, he'd had an idea.

Rob declared the public ferries too unreliable to use, and said planes too were questionable with erratic island weather.

He convinced the entire team that he needed to rent a private ship to transport them from Seattle to Friday Harbor.

Rick agreed, and then Rob simply gave the captain an extra five hundred dollars to pretend the ship had broken down in the middle of the ocean.

It worked like a charm. No one suspected a thing. The captain had even set off some sort of a smoke bomb, scaring the team into submission for a full hour before their complaints started.

Now Rob was finally in the clear. He gave the captain a signal that it was okay to restart, and off they went. Rob pretended they still had a chance to make the meeting, but by the time they docked in Friday Harbor, a call came in from Rick.

Rob answered as he watched the team shuffle down the dock. "Hello?"

"You blew it!"

He smiled. "Hey boss."

"Do you have any idea how much money you've wasted?"

"I'm sure we can – "

"No, there's no way. You missed the hearing. I can't believe I'm saying this, but you missed it. Where's your ship now, Rob?"

"We had some mechanical difficulties," he said evenly. "We can get another chance."

"No. Not for you. You're fired. You'll never work in finance again. You're a bum, do you know that? A bum!"

A bum! Rob had been called worse.

He couldn't stop smiling. Rick was livid. It confirmed what Rob had hoped for – the deal was really dead. The hotel was safe.

The line went dead, and Rob spent the rest of the trip chatting with the captain. When they arrived, he thanked the captain for his help and walked off of the ship into Friday Harbor.

For a moment he considered going to look for Lucy, but he decided against it. She would be surrounded by family and friends, of which he was neither.

Instead, he took an hour to walk around the shops in town before catching a ferry back to Orcas Island.

He'd left his car at the ferry terminal, half afraid Rick might try to repossess it out from under him. Luckily, no one had found it yet.

Rob drove back into Eastsound and spent two hours cleaning out his office. His landlord didn't care what he left behind, as long as the rent was paid through the end of the month. The desk and two chairs were Rob's gift to him.

He went back to his apartment, debating if he should try to contact Lucy one last time. She'd ignored all of his calls and texts for days, but last night, she'd finally responded. He'd texted one last apology before the hearing: "I'm so sorry about everything. And I really hope you guys win tomorrow."

Her reply had come quickly. "Yeah, sure. Don't ever speak to me again."

Rob pulled up her message and stared at the words. She had been pretty clear. She wanted nothing to do with him.

What was done was done. He needed to respect what she said and find a way to live with the choices he'd made.

He'd lost Lucy – deservedly so – along with his job, his father's respect, and his future in finance.

The silver lining was that he'd finally figured out what was important to him, even if it was realized too late.

He was thankful, at least, that he'd managed to stop OSS from taking over the hotel. It left him with a shred of something – honor, or maybe dignity, he wasn't sure – but he'd need it wherever he was going.

He would rebuild his life from the ground up, based on whatever bit of truth he'd finally uncovered. It was time to start over and leave the island in peace at last.

Chapter Twenty-nine

That evening's celebration was at The Grand Madrona Hotel. Chip cheerfully invited everyone who had played a role in saving the hotel – their lawyer, Margie and her crew, the landscaping team, and his friend who had showed up on short notice with a dump truck and a stump grinder. He'd invited the council members, too, but they politely declined.

The result was the hotel restaurant overflowing with good food, bottomless drinks, and roaring laughter.

Lillian was having a blast. She sat at one of the smaller tables, regaled by Chip's retelling of how he'd almost fallen into an abandoned well on one of the properties.

"That was your own fault," his stump grinding friend countered.

"You were supposed to warn me!" Chip yelled. He tried to look angry, but he was too happy. He had a goofy, non-Chip smile on his face.

"What more warning do you need than, 'Don't go over there, I don't think the well is covered'?"

Chip laughed, shaking his head. "I can't listen to everything you say. You talk too much."

"Yeah right!"

"You would've left me down there, too," Chip added.

His friend thought on this for a moment. "Yeah, I would have."

The table erupted into laughter and at that moment, Claire walked over and put her hands on Chip's shoulders. "What's so funny?"

He turned around, beaming up at her. "Everyone's enjoying the fact that your boyfriend almost fell into a well."

She let out a *tsk*. "That's awful!"

Chip stood and put his arm around her shoulders. "You know, the worst part of that story is having to use the word 'boyfriend.'"

"Is it? Worse than falling in a well?"

"We're too old for that word, don't you think?"

In an instant, Chip dropped down to one knee and pulled a violet box from his pocket.

Lillian gasped, and everyone around them fell silent.

"Claire, I kept trying to plan the perfect night to do this, and all I learned is that I'm terrible at planning."

She laughed, a hand over her mouth, but said nothing.

He continued. "Maybe there is no perfect moment, because who knows how long we have until the next terrible thing happens. But it doesn't matter, because you're perfect, and I know that no matter what life throws at us, we can handle anything together."

Chip popped the box open. Inside was a brilliant, deep-blue sapphire set in a filigree ring.

Lillian could feel herself choking up. Claire *loved* sapphires.

"I promise to stay away from all abandoned wells if you do me the honor of being my wife."

There were tears in her eyes as she put both hands on his face. "Yes, of course!"

Chip slipped the ring onto her finger before standing and planting a kiss square on her lips.

Lillian stood with her mouth hanging open, too stunned to notice Lucy dropping into the seat next to her.

"They're kissing, *gross*," Lucy whispered.

Lillian turned and elbowed her in the ribs. "Stop!"

"I'm just kidding," she said, beaming. "Let's go tell Claire we're happy to be her bridesmaids."

They managed to break through the small crowd that had formed around Chip and Claire to congratulate them both.

"You girls aren't upset?" Claire asked in a low voice.

"No!" Lillian couldn't believe she'd even think that. "We are so happy for you."

"What about Rose? Do you think she'll feel like – "

"Rose will be thrilled," Lillian said firmly. Of that she could be sure. She knew her twin sister better than anyone in the world.

"Yeah," Lucy added. "You know, I've always thought Chip would make a great stepdad."

Chip turned to her, still with that goofy smile on his face. "Why do I feel like an insult is lurking behind that comment?"

Lucy smiled and shook her head. "I'm not joking. You make Claire happy, and you even got her to the hospital. I respect that. Though I do expect more updates on her health in the future."

"You got it."

"Plus," she said slowly, "I like tormenting you, so now that you're family, I can kick it up a notch."

Lillian shot her a look, but everyone was already laughing, taking no ill will from her words.

They chatted a bit longer before it was too difficult to monopolize the happy couple – the rest of the dinner guests caught on to what had happened and were pushing in to give their congratulations.

Lillian and Lucy returned to their seats.

"I did not see that coming," Lillian said. "But I really do think it's great. Mom has never been happier."

Lucy nodded. "Agreed. Though I had someone else on my bingo card for getting engaged this year."

"Who?" Lillian turned to her, keeping her facial expression neutral. "You?"

Lucy rolled her eyes. "Yeah, right. I meant you, of course."

She looked away. She'd known what she'd meant. Lillian didn't feel like talking about it. "Right."

"I thought Mason was hinting this was the year?"

Lillian shrugged. "He was. I mean, he is."

"Don't sound so excited."

"We've been together so long that it won't really change anything," Lillian said evenly. "Engagements shouldn't be exciting. It's just the next step."

"Oh come on!" Lucy bumped her with her shoulder. "You have to be excited about the person you're going to spend your life with! Look at Chip. Look at how his grumpy face transformed."

Chip did look especially jovial. Lillian sighed. "I don't know. Maybe when Mason proposes I'll be excited too."

Lucy put her hand on her shoulder. "I hope so. I don't think anyone could deserve you, but I hope they make you light up like that. That's passion."

"Is passion a good thing?" Lillian turned to face her. It was a genuine question.

"Of course it is. Don't confuse passion with drama. Drama isn't good, but passion – passion is everything!"

It made sense for Lucy to think passion was everything. She lived her life like that, jumping from one thing to the next.

Lillian was different. She always had been. She was the sensible sister, and she was okay with that. Not everyone could chase their whims. "Is that what you had with Rob? Drama? Or was it passion?"

"It was neither." Lucy sat back in her chair and rubbed her eyes. "He was an illusion. There was nothing real about him."

"I don't believe that. It seems like he didn't follow through, you know. He didn't come to the hearing."

"Maybe he fell in a well," Lucy said simply.

Lillian was about to answer when she felt her phone vibrating in her pocket. It was Mason. "I'm sorry. I promised I'd talk to him tonight."

"Okay, but don't take too long or you'll miss the party."

Lillian nodded and stood from her seat. "Sure."

That was something she and Mason could work on – they could inject some passion into their relationship. She'd talk to him about it, and they could work on it together.

She took a few steps away from the crowd before answering the call. "Hey! I miss your handsome face."

"What?" His voice was loud, too loud, through the microphone. "What's going on over there? Aren't you home yet?"

She made it outside and away from the noise. "We had dinner, but now everyone's having fun. Guess what?"

"What?"

"My mom just got engaged!"

His tone softened. "Wow, cool. Tell her I said congratulations."

"I will. How're you?"

"Not bad. Work's been rough."

"Ah." She looked up. It was a cloudy night, but she could still make out some stars.

"How is that going to work?" he asked.

"What do you mean?"

"Your mom's engagement. What about us getting engaged? Is that going to get in the way?"

Lillian bit her lip. "I don't see why it would."

"Is it going to be another excuse for you to push our wedding off?"

"Of course not." She shut her eyes. Always the same arguments. "I was just excited to tell you about it. She's so happy."

He grunted. "Okay. Sorry. I'm in a bad mood. Maybe we can talk tomorrow."

"I think that's a good idea."

They ended the call and Lillian stood there, listening to the water lapping at the shore. She tried to envision Mason kneeling in front of her with the ring in his hand.

What would he say? What would *she* say?

Of course she'd tell him yes. They'd been planning this for years. It was the next step, the right step.

Yet, try as she might, she couldn't shake the feeling of unease in her chest.

Chapter Thirty

Lucy was left to grapple with Lillian's comments on her own, and it didn't take her long to decide there was no way Rob had inspired "passion" in her.

How could all that bickering have been passion? She couldn't stand the guy, from his stupid suits to his expensive cologne and even the way he smiled off to one side. He drove her crazy, always popping into her head with his unwelcome comments and opinions.

Even now, she couldn't stop thinking about him. It was infuriating. She wanted nothing to do with him.

Maybe Lillian was right. Maybe it was time for Lucy to get a boyfriend to be bored of, too.

One of Lillian's comments had really stuck, though. Why hadn't Rob come to the hearing? At first, Lucy hadn't given it much thought. She was relieved to not have to face him, and thrilled the hotel wasn't going to be taken.

It was unlike him to miss something important, though. He was always on time. Annoyingly so. Had something bad happened to him?

Dread, that old familiar lead blanket, settled onto Lucy's chest. It made no sense for Rob to disappear like that. What if there had been foul play? What if his plane had crashed? Lucy hadn't heard of any recently, but he could've been flying back to New York...

Just as Lucy's spiral began, Lillian reappeared.

"Are you okay?" she asked.

Lucy forced a smile. "Yeah, everything's fine. How's Mason?"

"He's fine."

"That's good." Lucy paused, then clapped her hands together. "Hey, do you want to go and egg Rob's office?"

A smile danced onto Lillian's lips. "What? Why?"

Lucy looked at her watch. It was late, so he might not be there. But there was a chance. "To teach him a lesson."

Lillian stared at her for a moment. "You just want to see him again, don't you?"

"No!" Lucy froze. She knew she'd answered too quickly.

"You don't have to lie to me."

"I'm not lying to you," Lucy said.

"Or..." Lillian smiled. "To yourself."

Rude. Lillian was being so rude today. What had gotten into her? "That's not what's happening."

"Oh Lucy, come on. It's obvious you still like him. Why don't you just talk to him? Figure out what happened."

"I don't like him," Lucy insisted. "I'm just worried about him."

"For you, worrying and liking are the same thing."

"What's that supposed to mean?"

"It's not bad. You just worry about the people you care about."

Lucy scoffed. "So now I care about him? This has escalated."

Lillian laughed, picking at the garlic bread on the table. "It's like what you do with Mom. You love her so much that you convinced yourself she was going to die."

"I mean, she *is* going to die. We all are."

"Yes, but you were convinced she was sick, even though she wasn't."

Lucy frowned. There was still no way to be sure Claire wasn't sick. Sure, she had been fine for a few weeks, but what did that mean? Her illness could still be lurking beneath the surface. "That has nothing to do with Rob."

Lillian put a hand on top of Lucy's. "I know. It has to do with Mom and Dad."

"Here we go!" Lucy said. "You're trying to analyze me like Rob did."

Lillian's eyes lit up. "What did he say? Is that why you're so angry with him?"

"No, I'm angry because he tried to steal the hotel out from under us and lied to my face."

"Ah, right. What else did he say to you?"

Lucy let out a huff and repeated the words that had been echoing in her head for the past few days: she couldn't put down roots, and all she did was run away and look for distractions.

When she was finished, Lillian stared at her, saying nothing.

"What?" Lucy asked. "Don't tell me you agree with him."

"I mean...do you not? It's not really a secret that you change your mind a lot," Lillian said delicately.

"Well that's – when I change my mind – it's because I don't – "

"Does putting down roots scare you?" Lillian dropped her voice. "Or does loving someone make you scared, because you only think about losing them?"

Lucy's mouth popped open. "I can't believe you think that of me! That's not what it is. I'm just – I don't know. This is how I am."

Lillian put her hands up in surrender. "Okay. I'm sorry."

Lucy wasn't done with the conversation. "And what does that have to do with Mom and Dad dying in a plane crash? That was thirty years ago. I'm not living like, scared, because of that."

"I'm not saying you are!" She leaned forward and took a deep breath. "I just think when you lose something so important, there are lingering effects. It's not like Rose and I are unaffected by it. We're all affected in different ways. I just – I don't want it to hold you back from living."

"I'm living just fine, thank you." Lucy leaned back and looked around. The party was starting to die off. "Should we get a glass of champagne before they close the bar?"

Lillian smiled. "Sure."

The reveling didn't last much longer and the restaurant staff started closing up. Marty gave them a ride home, and, thankfully, Lillian didn't try to analyze Lucy again.

Lucy's paranoia got the best of her, though, and that night before she went to bed, she sent a text to Rob. "Not that I really care, but I just wanted to make sure you're okay. You never showed today."

She sent the text and waited a few minutes. Ten. Fifteen. Forty-five.

How was she supposed to fall asleep if he wouldn't answer?

A cold feeling washed over her. Just because she was mad at him didn't mean she wanted something bad to happen to him.

She fell asleep eventually, but in the morning there was still no message from him. Lucy waited until she was in her car driving to work to give him a call.

The phone rang endlessly, and she was just about to hang up when his voice broke through.

"Lucy?"

Shoot.

He was alive!

Chapter Thirty-one

He strained to listen. "Hello? Are you there?"
There was only rustling from her side of the call. Maybe she'd butt dialed him.

No. He didn't believe that. Something had to be very wrong for her to call. Maybe OSS had found a loophole? Was there going to be another hearing?

"Is everything okay?" he asked.

"What?" More rustling. "Yeah, I'm fine. I wanted to see if – I mean, are you okay?"

"Yes. Why?"

Silence hung between them for a moment before Lucy spoke again. "I thought it was weird when I didn't see you at the hearing yesterday. I thought something might've happened to you."

His heart fluttered. Was Lucy...concerned about him? "No, nothing like that. I, uh, took a page out of your playbook, actually."

"I don't have a playbook."

Rob grinned. He didn't mind her hostility if she was talking to him again. He was desperate to keep her on the line. "I told all of OSS's lawyers and experts that I'd get them to the hearing on time and booked a private ship."

"And then left them out at sea?"

"Basically." He laughed, then picked up his pace. "I paid the captain to pretend the ship was broken down. We drifted around the Strait of Juan de Fuca until the hearing was over."

Silence on her end.

He spoke again. "It kept them away. It seemed like something you would do."

Silence for a moment, then, "Huh. Not bad."

Rob started to say, "Listen, I'm – " at the same moment she said "Okay, I guess – "

He stopped. "I'm sorry. You go ahead."

"No. What were you saying?"

He cleared his throat. "I just need to reiterate how sorry I am about everything. I wanted to apologize before, and I know I can't make up for what happened. I won't deny my role in targeting the hotel. I came up with the idea, but then – "

"*You* came up with the idea!" She let out a disgusted sigh.

"I know." He cringed and shut his eyes. "That was before I knew you, and before I knew anything about this place. I didn't know Claire owned the hotel. Once I found out, I did everything in my power to undo it."

She was quiet for a beat. "I see."

"There's no excuse for what I did." he added. "I wish it had never happened, but..." If only he'd had time to practice this. He should've written something down, gotten his thoughts straight. It was a surprise she was willing to speak to him, though, and he couldn't lose his chance. He needed to press on. "I'm glad I met you."

"Okay." Lucy shuffled around. "Are you at your office?"

Ouch. Clearly she wasn't ready to forgive him yet. Perhaps she never would be. "No. I'm at the Orcas airport. I'm getting a flight to Seattle, then back to New York."

"Oh!" The amusement was back in her voice. "Did you get in trouble at the office?"

"You could say that. I was fired, as expected, and my boss managed to take the car almost immediately. So that was nice."

Lucy let out a laugh. "How did you get to the airport?"

"My neighbor gave me a ride. It's funny. I'm just realizing that people here are actually pretty nice."

"That is funny," she said. "I've noticed that myself."

"I bet."

"I have to get to work," she said. "Good luck with your flight. Hope you don't die."

He stared down at the ground, smiling to himself. "Do you mean that?"

"Of course." She let out a little laugh. "Take care."

He took a breath, hoping to say more, hoping to fix what he'd done.

But there was nothing left to say. He'd gotten to tell her the truth, at least, and he'd have to leave it at that. "Goodbye, Lucy."

Rob ended the call, staring at the floor in front of him. The plastic airport chair wasn't particularly comfortable, and now that he was off the phone, he realized how stiff his muscles had been throughout the conversation.

He took a deep breath and released the tension, a hollow feeling settling into his chest.

So that was the last time he'd ever speak to Lucy, wasn't it? It seemed odd. Only a few weeks ago, he was on track to get everything he'd ever wanted. He was sure of himself, sure of his choices.

Then this beautiful and ferocious redhead blazed into his life with a scowl and a heart full of fire. He felt as though he'd been sitting at a neatly set table and she showed up, out of nowhere, and flipped it over for a laugh.

That was Lucy. If he'd opened his eyes sooner, maybe he wouldn't have lost his chance with her. Maybe he would've been lucky enough to have that chaos, that energy in his life every day – questioning him, teasing him, challenging him to be a better person.

His flight started boarding. Rob stood and stretched the tightness out of his shoulders. It was time to take Lucy's last advice – to try not to die.

He smiled as he got in line.

Chapter Thirty-two

Getting off the phone with Rob wasn't quite the balm to Lucy's nerves she hoped it would be. After restocking the egg display, she flitted from one side of the shop to the other, trying to come up with something to do. There were emails to answer and online orders to fill, and she set her mind to attending to that.

Annoyingly, all of those tasks only took half an hour, leaving her time to think.

Lucy could kick herself for calling Rob. Why had she worked herself into thinking he'd been hurt? Lillian's words now haunted her, along with the biting comments he'd made. Could everyone see her so clearly? Was she really just running from everything and everyone?

After an hour of hemming and hawing, Lucy finally broke down and called Lillian.

"Hey," Lucy said gruffly.

"Hey! How's it going?"

"Everything's fine. I just wanted you to know I talked to Rob."

"Rob?" Lillian paused. "And? What did he say?"

Lucy waved a hand. "Lots of stuff. I don't know. He was nice. He said he was sorry, but the important thing is that he's okay."

"Right. Of course."

Lucy fiddled with her pen and the clip snapped off into her hand. "Yeah."

"Is something the matter?"

She stood from her stool, then sat, then stood again before walking to look out the window. There were no customers coming. She had time to talk. "He's about to fly out. He's leaving."

"Oh. How does that make you feel?"

"Worried!" Lucy let out a nervous laugh. "What if his plane goes down? I told him not to die, but I probably should've addressed if I forgive him or not, just in case. He kept OSS away from the hearing."

"Wow. Do you forgive him?"

Lucy sat down again. "I don't know."

He'd admitted it was his idea to target the hotel. That was unforgivable!

On the other hand, he'd also held a bunch of lawyers and experts hostage at sea to keep them from getting to the hearing. That meant something. That had to mean something...

"Lucy? Are you still there?"

Lillian was going to try to analyze her again if she didn't come up with something. "Sorry. I was just thinking."

"I have a question for you," Lillian said.

"Okay."

"How would you feel if his plane did go down? Just bam! Right into the ocean?"

A pit opened in her stomach. "I'd feel awful! I don't want him to die!"

Lillian laughed. "Right. I don't mean that. Would you regret not telling him how you feel?"

Lucy opened her mouth to answer, then hesitated. Her knee-jerk reaction was to say she didn't know how she felt, but that wasn't going to cut it.

The thought of his plane going down was, of course, horrifying, and Lucy's worst fear.

If he did die, however, she wouldn't be thinking about how he'd gone after the hotel. She'd think of him struggling to eat an oyster, or of him trying to convince her not to run off on a cruise ship, or the way his lips found hers in the shining moonlight on the ship...

"I don't want him to leave," Lucy said, her voice cracking.

"Tell him that."

"I can't." Lucy's voice was high, almost a whine.

"You can," Lillian said gently. "You can be afraid and still do what needs to be done."

She was going to say she wasn't afraid, but that was a lie. She wasn't sure why it was a lie, but it was.

There was a primal fear deep in the pit of her stomach, one that made her nauseous and cold, one that was trying to convince her she would not be okay unless she stayed far away from Rob.

At the same time, there was a longing in her heart, a softer, squishier feeling, pulling her in and promising everything good – ice cream, baby goats hopping, hand holding while walking alongside the ocean at sunset…

Lucy took a deep breath. "I don't know if I can do it."

"Yes you can," Lillian said. "I believe in you."

She rubbed her face. It seemed impossible. Her gut was telling her to run, but her heart felt sick over the idea of never seeing him again. How was she supposed to sort this out? "Maybe I'll just go and say hello. Catch him before his flight."

"Good idea!"

She ended the call and immediately dialed Rob. The phone rang and rang before hitting his voicemail.

"Hi, you've reached Rob Coolidge. I can't get to the phone right now, but if you leave your name and number – "

She hung up. She wasn't ready to leave a voicemail. She had no idea what to say to him.

It'd be better to give her message in person. She could pop over to the airport and come up with something to say on the drive. Fiona wouldn't mind if she took a little break. They'd been slow all day.

Now wasn't the time to think or second-guess. Lucy grabbed her coat, locked the farm shop door, and sent a message to Fiona. "I have to run, but I'll be back soon. Sorry!"

Her heart pounded in her chest as she got to her car. It didn't feel quite like facing her fears – maybe running along-side them. That was good enough for now, as long as she kept moving.

The airport in Eastsound had a sleepy, empty parking lot running along the landing strip. Lucy got out of her car and eyed the small planes sitting nearby, baking in the sun.

Were these the broken ones? Why were they just sitting out like that? How often did they break down? How often did the white paint blind the pilots and cause crashes?

Lucy shuddered. This was a dangerous place, one she would never come to unless she was experiencing the sort of madness she felt now.

She walked past the plane deathtraps and through the front door of the airport. It was less of an airport and more of a large room. There was only one other person inside, and disappointingly, he didn't look like Rob at all.

"Hi, I was wondering – "

The man's mouth popped open. "You're Lucy Woodley, aren't you?"

She paused, smiling reflexively. "Yes."

He rushed around the counter to shake her hand. "I watched you at the council meeting and read about how you saved Grindstone. I'm a huge fan."

Now there was something she hadn't expected – she was a bonafide island celebrity. "Thank you!" she said, beaming. "That's very nice of you. I've never had a fan before."

He laughed heartily. "We were all impressed with what you've done around here. Really, just wonderful."

"You know, I'm here to serve."

He laughed again. "I'm sorry for gushing like this. Is there something I can help you with today?"

"Yes, I was looking for a friend of mine. His name is Rob. I think he's flying to Seattle?"

The man made a face. "Well, he might've been on the flight that just went out of here a half hour ago."

Her heart sank. "A half hour, huh? So he's gone?"

"Afraid so. Did you need to catch up with him?"

"No – I mean, yes, but I can try to find him another time."

The man rushed around to get back to his computer. "We have another flight going out this afternoon."

Her manic mind was annoyed by this bump in the road, but she wouldn't be stopped. She could get on a ferry and be in Seattle in, oh, five or six hours. "That's all right. Thanks for your help."

He held up a finger and tapped the keyboard with his other hand. "There's a seaplane going out of Deer Harbor in twenty minutes. I'm happy to give you a discount."

A seaplane?

Absolutely not. "No, thank you, I could never – "

"I insist. It looks like there's one seat left. I'll give it to you for fifty bucks. How's that?"

"That's really okay – "

"Okay, okay!" He grinned, clicking around the screen. "You talked me down. Twenty-five dollars, but only because you're a hero around here."

Lucy wanted to tell him he couldn't pay her to get on that plane, but somehow the glow of celebrity had stunned her.

"Can I see your license?" he asked.

She numbly pulled her wallet out of her purse and handed the entire thing over. He accepted it, propping it open to look at her driver's license.

"How would you like to pay?" he asked.

"Credit, I think." She reached forward and pulled out one of her many credit cards.

He smiled, ran it through a machine, and got back to typing. Lucy watched, afraid to say another word in case he offered her something else.

After returning her wallet, he fetched the small printed ticket. "Here you go. I'll give them a call to let them know you're on the way. They'll wait for you."

Lucy clutched the ticket in her sweaty palm and forced a smile. "Thank you so much!"

There was no way she was going on a plane, let alone one that landed on water, but she wasn't going to break the poor man's heart. She went out to her car with the full intention of running away and never facing this sweet man again.

She started her car and pulled out of her spot, relieved to be getting away from the looming planes. When she got to the end of the road, she debated turning left to get back to work, or right to go to Deer Harbor. She figured she should at least swing by the seaplane and let the pilot know she wasn't getting on.

Yeah, that would be fine. She didn't want to ruin her reputation as a local celebrity so quickly.

At the harbor, there was only one seaplane bobbing in the water. They were probably annoyed about waiting for her, so she hastily parked and ran down.

"I'm sorry, I just – "

"There she is!" yelled a man. "Come on board, Lucy. I saved the front seat for you."

"Oh no, that's okay, I was just coming to let you know I won't be – "

"Don't be shy," the man said, offering her a hand as he pulled open the passenger door.

There were two other women on the plane, and they too waved her on.

"It's so nice to meet you, Lucy!" one of the women said.

"I *love* The Grand Madrona. Claire comes into my tea shop, and I was horrified to hear about that condemnation."

Lucy smiled, nodded, and said hello, trying her best to seem like a normal human.

But she didn't feel like a normal human. This was a nightmare. She must've fallen asleep. She wasn't actually on a plane. The pilot wasn't closing the door. He wasn't handing her a headset.

This was not happening!

Except it most certainly was.

Chapter Thirty-three

H is flight landed at the King County Airport. It was much larger than the airport on Orcas, but still small compared to the Seattle-Tacoma International Airport he was headed to next.

It felt like he was taking baby steps into his new life. First Seattle, then New York, then...what?

An adventure, apparently.

Rob turned his phone on once he got into the terminal and saw he had a missed call from Lucy.

Hope bubbled in his chest. He'd spent the entire flight thinking about her, regretting what he'd failed to say. There was so much, and he'd just left it like a bumbling fool.

Was there a chance he'd said something intelligible enough for her to want to keep the lines of communication open?

He quickly tried calling her back, but no response. He tapped out a message. "Sorry I missed your call. I did decide to take your advice and not die. I'm in Seattle, on my way to SEATAC now, but feel free to call any time."

After hitting send, he regretted his last comment. It made him sound like he was trying to sell her something.

In a way he was trying to sell something: himself. Until recently, he'd been quite good at it. Now he had the task of rebuilding who he was. There was bound to be some awkwardness.

Rob hadn't thought of how to get to the Seattle airport, and in his excitement about Lucy, made the mistake of getting into a cab. Only after he was stuck in bumper-to-bumper traffic did he do an online search and realize he could've taken the light rail and saved himself a lot of time and money.

Oh well. This was new Rob, apparently, and he needed to slow down and take the time to look around.

When he finally got to the airport, he paid the hefty taxi bill, hauled his bag out of the trunk, and walked into the terminal. He still hadn't heard from Lucy – she might keep him waiting all day, and he was fine with that, as long as she called him back eventually.

The airport was busy and pleasantly distracting. There were people from all walks of life – students in rowdy groups and couples chasing down their small kids like escaped geese. There were older couples, too, in matching outfits, and younger couples displaying far too much public affection.

Actually, the more he looked around, it seemed like it was almost all couples. Rob stood and stared. It had never bothered him to travel alone before, but now it really struck him.

He was alone. Completely alone. No one wanted to go on a trip with him. There wasn't even anyone who wanted to wear matching Costco cargo shorts with him.

How long had he planned to live his life alone like this? Why had he let it go on so long?

It wasn't until Lucy had practically smacked him in the face that he'd woken up. This was another thing to add to the list. New job, new lifestyle, new outlook on love.

He got into the security line and inched forward, continuing his game of people watching. If Lucy were here, he could tell her the stories he was making up about everyone nearby.

The tired looking couple was on the way to their honeymoon after an exhausting wedding with pushy relatives. The two next to him weren't speaking because the guy had dropped his wife's toothbrush in the toilet that morning and refused to apologize, telling her it was her fault for leaving it so close to the bowl.

He smiled at that one. Lucy would've liked it. It seemed like an argument they could've gotten into one day, if he hadn't ruined everything. He was staring off, daydreaming, when he felt a tap on his shoulder.

Rob startled and turned around. "I think someone's trying to get your attention," said the woman behind him whom he'd decided was traveling to a sandcastle-building competition.

"Oh, thanks." Rob looked where she was pointing and had to do a double take. It was a woman who looked just like Lucy.

No – it was Lucy!

He waved at her before stumbling out of line.

"What are you doing here?" he asked when he reached her.

"I could ask you the same question," she said, hands on her hips.

He grinned at her, probably looking like a total idiot. He didn't care. "I'm going back home."

"I need to talk to you." She grabbed him by the wrist with surprising force. "Let's talk over here."

He was so dumbfounded that he'd left his bag behind for a few seconds. After retreating to grab it, he joined Lucy at a small table near a coffee shop.

"I can't believe you're here," he said. It was as though he'd imagined her into being.

"I can't believe I am either." She shook her head. "They put me on a *seaplane*."

His mouth dropped open. "They did what?"

She slapped a hand to her forehead. "It was all because this guy liked me at the airport and I didn't know how to say no and – it doesn't matter. But you know we landed on a lake? And then I – "

"Hang on, you *flew* here?"

She nodded. "I think I did. Yes."

A smile spread across his face. "And you didn't die?"

"Not this time, though I thought I was going to. I think I still might, actually." She took a shaky breath and looked down at her hands.

"I think you'll be okay." He stared at her, studying the gentle curve of her lips and her slightly tousled hair. It felt like he hadn't seen her in years. He was starved for every detail.

"So, going back to what you said. You got fired?"

He nodded.

"Because you sacrificed your very important career to save the hotel?"

"It's not a very important career," he said. "But yes."

She sat back and crossed her arms. "Do you promise you'll never do it again?"

He tried not to smile. As if he would ever consider it. "Of course."

"Say it."

He leaned forward. "I promise I will never try to use eminent domain on The Grand Madrona Hotel again."

"Or anyplace else!" she said, holding up a finger.

"Or anywhere else." He clasped his hands in front of him. It was too hard not to smile, but he was trying to be serious. "Those days are behind me."

"You just changed your mind like that?" Lucy asked. "Are you sure this new plan isn't just some...distraction?"

He could feel his face getting hot. He looked down for a moment, then back into her eyes. "I'm sorry I said those things. It was mean and petty – "

She cut him off. "And true." Lucy let out a sigh. "I think I do look for distractions, and I do run from things. You weren't wrong."

"Neither were you," he said. "I'm a leech. Well, I was. Now I don't know what I am."

"You can only go up from there," she offered.

He let out a laugh. "Right. You know, it's not easy for me."

"To not be a leech?"

She was smiling now, and Rob had to force himself to focus. It was hard to do when she just swooped in like that.

"No," he said, "To change course. I have a lot of years of being wrong behind me. It took some harsh words to realize it, but I get it now."

"Meanwhile, I'll change course whenever the wind blows." Lucy bit her lip. "We're sort of a perfect match, aren't we?"

A breath caught in his chest. "I've always thought so, yes."

She nodded and slowly leaned forward, reaching for one of his hands. "I've been thinking a lot recently, and I decided I don't want you to leave." She flinched. "I think I like you."

He gripped her hand in his. Her tiny fingers were cold and clammy, likely a lingering effect from her flight. Or perhaps from what she'd said.

"That's good." He dropped his voice. "Because I think I'm in love with you."

She gasped. "Robert! You can't just tell a girl you're in love with her in the middle of an airport."

"Yes I can, especially when she almost died getting here."

Her stern expression melted into a laugh, and she hid her eyes behind one hand. "I really did almost die."

He stood from his chair and knelt next to her, placing a delicate kiss on the back of her hand. "Can I help you get home safely, then?"

She shrugged. "I guess so."

He leaned forward and broke his grin to kiss her.

Epilogue

It was the thirty-year anniversary of the plane crash, and Lillian was surprised by how weepy she felt.

"Come on. Don't go falling apart on me now," Lucy said, stopping to apply some lipstick in the mirror. "We have to hold it together for Claire."

She took a deep breath and nodded. "You're right. It's just..." Her voice cracked, and she couldn't finish her sentence.

Lucy turned to her. "Aw, Lillian!" She wrapped her arms around her and squeezed tightly. "It's okay. Let it out."

A hiccup caught in her throat, and after another deep breath, she felt like she could speak again. "It's just crazy to think about how long it's been, but at the same time, it feels like it hasn't been long at all."

"Yeah," Lucy said. "It has been a while though. Thirty years. But now we're all together – you, me, Mom, and Rose. Even Aunt Becca made her way back!"

Lillian tried to wriggle out of Lucy's grip, but she wouldn't let go. Just then, Rose emerged from the bathroom. "Am I missing a group hug?"

"No, I was just saying how – " Lillian felt another sob coming on and forced herself to take a deep breath.

"Aw, Lil! Don't cry." Rose wrapped her arms around them both and squeezed tight. "It's going to be such a nice day."

"I know," Lillian warbled, "I'm glad we're all here."

She felt ridiculous, but there was no point in trying to stop it. Lillian let out a few sobs and after a minute, she blew her nose, regained her composure, and they headed for the car.

Their first stop was to pick up Claire and Aunt Becca.

As soon as they pulled up to the house, Becca flung the door open and waved madly.

She had on a typically bright outfit – a red flowing skirt, a tie-dyed tank top under a furry looking coat, and a yellow straw hat, the brim flopping in front of her eyes.

Becca ran toward the car, her flip flops clapping with each step, and Claire followed, dressed in a white linen dress and a wool coat.

"I've got snacks in my bag," Becca said as she crammed into the car. "Anyone hungry?"

Lucy snorted a laugh. "There's going to be food on the boat."

Becca ignored her, reaching into the bag and pulling out a handful of candy bars. "And we're supposed to trust that? What if we get lost at sea?"

Lillian and Rose erupted into laughter, just as Claire shimmied her way into the car.

"Is there enough room for me?" Claire asked, hanging halfway off of the seat.

"Of course! Move your butt, Rose!" Becca barked, shoving her over.

Lillian couldn't stop laughing, and the morose cloud that had been following her all morning dissipated.

Once everyone was safely buckled in, Lucy put the car into drive and headed toward the harbor. Rob, who had proven to be an extremely attentive boyfriend, had rented out an entire sailboat for their day. The plan was to sail around the San Juan Islands looking at wildlife, enjoying brunch and dinner, and having cocktails – alcohol-free ones for Aunt Becca, of course.

Lillian was impressed with Rob's planning skills. After he'd come up with the idea, he hand-picked the meals and found a schedule to accommodate each of them.

Mason couldn't come up with something that thoughtful if his life depended on it.

Not that it was a competition. Lillian wasn't a competitive person; she was just impressed with Rob. Somehow, he'd managed to break through Lucy's quite formidable walls, all while managing to get her to face some of her more destructive habits.

For now, Lucy was still working at the farm. She was quite beloved there, and rightfully so. She was taking her time figuring out what she wanted to do next – whether it was going back to school or setting herself up in a new career.

Most impressive to Lillian was the fact that Lucy was allowing herself to be crazy about Rob. She wasn't holding back, and she wasn't afraid.

Well, at least she wasn't afraid to show how she felt. Lucy was still afraid he'd die in a plane crash, or drive off a cliff, or drown when swimming in one of the lakes in the park. But those were normal Lucy fears, not ones that made her run away.

When they got to the harbor, the sight of the ship took Lillian's breath away. It was gorgeous, like something from a storybook or an antique, a ship in a bottle blown up to five hundred times its size.

The captain greeted them with a tray of fresh squeezed orange juices.

"I like this," Becca said. "But I was hoping you'd be dressed like a pirate."

"I'll get my eyepatch out, as long as you don't mind me steering one eyed."

"I don't mind!" she said, taking a swig of the juice.

Lucy shook her head. "He needs both eyes so he can spot eagles and orcas and all that stuff."

Claire laughed. "You have plenty of eyes between us to spot those."

It was a gorgeous day – the air was cool, but it felt pleasantly warm in the sun. The sky was a solid sheet of blue, and the water calm and inviting. They were giggling and exploring the deck when Lillian's phone rang.

It was Mason. She stepped away before answering. "Hey."

"Hey. I got back from my trip a few days early. Do you want to grab dinner tonight?"

There was a commotion behind her –Becca had tried to untie a rope and was quickly caught by the captain.

Lillian stifled a laugh. "I can't. I'm still on the island."

He let out a heavy sigh. "We talked about this."

"I told you I wasn't ready to leave yet."

"And I told *you* that when I got home, I expected you to be here."

Lillian clenched her teeth. "You know you don't own me, right?"

"How am I supposed to propose to you if you're always running off to that island?"

"I'm not running off," she said firmly. Also, that sounded like a threat, one Lillian knew was a bluff. He never stopped talking about proposing. It was his idea, not hers. "Do you know what today is?"

"March twenty-ninth, which means you've been there for over a month and – "

"It's the anniversary of my parents' death. I'm here commemorating it with my mom, and my sisters, and my aunt."

He was quiet for a moment. "Oh."

He'd completely forgotten what day it was! And she'd thought he was calling to say something nice.

She waited, and instead of saying something nice he said, "So you're coming home after that? I leave again next week."

She had to resist the urge to chuck her phone into the glistening water below. "Do you expect me to always sit around waiting for you to come back from your business trips? Even after you've seen what it's like to be the one waiting?"

"It was never a problem for you before," he snapped. "If you're suddenly so unhappy, maybe we should break up."

She turned around to make sure no one was eavesdropping. Lucy was nearby, but she was distracted and giggling with Rose.

It wasn't unusual for Mason to threaten a breakup. He'd done it a handful of times over the years, usually when Lillian felt like she was at the end of her rope.

It always worked. The idea of losing him was too much, and she'd give in to whatever fight they were having.

Yet for some reason, this time was different. She was *tired*. She was sick of feeling dread whenever his name popped up on her phone. She couldn't help but notice how different things were for Lucy – she was bursting with excitement every time she saw Rob, even though she got furious at him at least once a week.

The week prior, Lillian and Lucy had been brainstorming ideas for their mom's wedding, and it dawned on Lillian that she was more excited to plan that wedding than her own.

Coming to Orcas Island had changed something within her. She'd been away long enough to gather her thoughts and her strength.

Lillian didn't want to spend her life waiting around for Mason. Nothing would ever be enough for him – enough money, a big enough house, nice enough cars.

Lillian didn't want any of that! She wanted to spend time with Lucy, and Rose, and her mom and Aunt Becca. She wanted a partner who was interested in her life, someone who not only remembered a day as important as the anniversary of her parents' death, but did something *nice* instead of scolding her.

She didn't want to wait for Mason anymore. She wanted to *live.*

"You're right," she said slowly, "I think we need to break up."

He let out a groan. "Oh stop. You don't mean it. You're just mad and trying to get your way."

"It's not my way, Mason." She lowered her voice. "Things obviously aren't working between us, so why are we doing this?"

"Things were working perfectly fine before!"

It was too quiet behind her. She turned and saw Lucy watching intently.

Oh well. She was getting a front row seat to the drama now.

"Yeah, things were fine before," Lillian said, trying to keep her voice even, "because I was the one making all of the sacrifices. I don't want to do that anymore."

"How many times do I have to tell you that everything I do is for you? All of my work stuff is for you, Lil. All the money I'm saving is for *us*. We need to be responsible about our future. You know this."

She wasn't going to get into this argument again. He refused to hear her, and finally, she was refusing to continue explaining herself. "I'm sorry, Mason, but it's over."

"Yeah, great. Whatever. Bye."

He disconnected the call and Lillian stood there, staring into the blue water. It looked so welcoming, but she knew the temperature had to be around fifty degrees.

Still, jumping in would feel less shocking than what she'd just done. Her body felt tingly, and her head was filled with air.

In an instant, Lucy was at her side. "Did you just do what I think you just did?"

She put her phone back into her pocket. "Yes."

Her eyes bulged. "Are you okay?"

"I will be." Lillian cautioned a smile. "Do you mind if I stay with you for a few months?"

"*Mind?*" Lucy jumped up and down, squealing. "That would be incredible!"

Rose came over, hands on her hips. "Am I being left out again? I'm going to have to move to this island soon."

"I've got room for everybody," Lucy said.

"Did I hear you're all moving to Orcas?" Claire asked, dragging Becca behind her by the wrist. "I would love that."

"I wish," Rose said. "Maybe soon."

Lillian bit her lip and smiled. "I'll be here for a while."

Claire clapped her hands together. "That's wonderful news!"

"I can't believe you did that," Lucy said, shaking her head.

Lillian shifted. "Yeah, I kind of can't believe I did either."

"You just broke up with him. Just like that!"

"It's about time," Rose said, a smile on her lips.

Lillian let out a sigh. "I guess I'm feeling spontaneous. Lucy is rubbing off on me."

They all laughed.

"Hey," Lucy protested, "that's not fair. You can't blame this on me. Don't act like this has nothing to do with Dustin."

"Dustin?" Lillian frowned.

"Who's Dustin?" asked Aunt Becca.

Before Lillian could answer, Rose cut in. "He was Lil's high school sweetheart."

"He *adored* her," Lucy added.

Claire nodded, shooting a sympathetic look at Lillian. "He really did. He proposed to her when they graduated, it was adorable."

"That's so sweet," Becca said, throwing a hand to her chest.

Lillian didn't blush easily, but she was starting to feel a heat rising in her cheeks. "Why would it have anything to do with Dustin?"

Lucy's face fell. "You didn't hear? Never mind."

Lillian would never admit it, but of course she had a vague idea of what Dustin had been up to. After she turned down his proposal all those years ago, he went on to live his dreams and became a veterinarian. Sometimes Lillian watched the educational videos he posted online – things like how to trim a dog's nails or how to get a cat in a carrier – even though she didn't have a pet. Mason was allergic to everything.

"We don't talk anymore," she said simply.

"Oh. Well, he was offered to host a TV show and is coming to the islands for it," Lucy said, looking around the group. "I thought everyone knew. It was on the news."

Lillian's stomach dropped. How had she missed that?

"Looks like we're not all as nosey as you," Rose said, jabbing Lucy in the side.

She laughed. "Well sorry, I guess I'm just a busybody."

Becca grunted, downing the rest of her orange juice. "How about you find a way for me to visit more often, Lucy. I don't think the captain will let me back on the island after I got tangled up in that rope."

They burst into laughter and the moment passed. Lillian was grateful to her aunt for changing the subject. She'd deal with Dustin later – if what Lucy had said was even happening.

"Oh wait!" Lucy snapped her fingers. "Rob said we're supposed to have some chocolate-covered strawberries before we start. I think they're downstairs..."

Everyone turned to follow, except for Lillian. She wanted a moment to herself.

She turned back to the water and hung her hands over the railing. Despite the events of the day, Lillian felt calm.

It was strange. She'd broken up with Mason, something she'd feared would happen for years. Yet to her surprise, she felt relieved.

On top of that, it was the anniversary of a terrible event. She'd lost her parents thirty years ago today, but she still had so much family around her. So much love.

Long ago, Lillian had found ways to make peace with her past, but this was the first time she was trying to make peace with her future. Though it was frightening, it felt right.

Lillian closed her eyes, enjoying the warmth of the sun on her face. Today was the right day for a new start.

The Next Chapter

Introduction to *Sunset Weddings*

Get ready for the fourth installment of the Orcas Island series! Lillian makes her move official, and her new life gets off to a rocky start when trouble rolls in like a bad storm.

She tries to keep herself busy with work and Claire's upcoming wedding, but Mason refuses to leave her in peace. He's convinced they're destined to walk down the aisle, and he's made up his mind to win her back. The only problem? Mason isn't the only one after her heart...

Sunset Weddings debuts March 2023. Pre-order your copy today!

Would you like to join my reader group?

Sign up for my reader newsletter and get a free copy of my novella Christmas at Saltwater Cove. You can sign up by visiting: https://bit.ly/XmasSWC

About the Author

Amelia Addler writes always sweet, always swoon-worthy romance stories and believes that everyone deserves their own happily ever after.

Her soulmate is a man who once spent five weeks driving her to work at 4AM after her car broke down (and he didn't complain, not even once). She is lucky enough to be married to that man and they live in Pittsburgh with their little yellow mutt. Visit her website at AmeliaAddler.com or drop her an email at amelia@AmeliaAddler.com.

Also by Amelia...

The Orcas Island Series
Sunset Cove

Sunset Secrets

Sunset Tides

Sunset Weddings

The Westcott Bay Series
Saltwater Cove

Saltwater Studios

Saltwater Secrets

Saltwater Crossing

Saltwater Falls

Saltwater Memories

Saltwater Promises

Christmas at Saltwater Cove

Standalone Novels
The Summer Request

The Billionaire Date Series

Made in the USA
Las Vegas, NV
21 March 2024

87542780R00152